HER HEART'S DESIRE

Callie headed for the stables to investigate the available tools. She found Tony there before her, garbed in a coat and buckskins that only by some miracle had been spared from a rubbish heap. He looked up at her approach, and a smile of pure enjoyment spread across his strained face.

It stopped Callie like a blow from a bouquet of roses, heady and intoxicating. There he was at last, her childhood idol, restored in spirit if not yet in body. Tall, rugged, handsome—and so much more. The deviltry danced once again in his eyes, the old energy suffused him, reaching out to wrap about her as well, to draw her into his web of laughter and enthusiasm.

She loved him. The certainty washed over her like a tidal wave. She loved him, utterly and completely. Too stunned to move, she simply gazed at him as her mind raced. What would happen, now that he was restored? Would he see in her a romantic princess in desperate need of a knight-errant to rescue her? Or would she remain in his eyes a little girl, capable and temper-driven, whom he would tease and dismiss? She held her breath, afraid to break the spell that enveloped h

The Matchmaking Ghost

Janice Bennett

Zebra Books
Kensington Publishing Corp.
http://www.zebrabooks.com

ZEBRA BOOKS are published by

Kensington Publishing Corp.
850 Third Avenue
New York, NY 10022

First Printing: April, 1998
10 9 8 7 6 5 4 3 2 1

Printed in the United States of America

For Susan. Thank you.

One

The prickling started along the back of his neck, like the sensations of a finger barely touching his skin. Nothing frightening, just the awareness of an otherworldly presence. It raised the tiny hairs along his nape, making him shiver with its sudden chill. At the fringes of his vision, the illusive ghostly flame flickered, then flared.

Captain Anthony, Lord Lambeth, spun from the window to bring the apparition fully into sight, but it vanished even as he moved. In the chair at his side, Marmaduke, the huge marmalade and white cat, relaxed from its rigid pose of feline intensity, licked its paw, and proceeded to smooth its quivering whiskers back into place. The morning's ghostly activity appeared to have come to an end.

But why, wondered Tony, had it occurred at all? The resident ghost of Lambeth Grange had indulged in an unusual amount of activity of late. Frowning, Tony contemplated the spacious breakfast parlor. Sunlight streamed through the window at his back, tracing delicate patterns across the silver and china settings for two on the mahogany table, and falling across the

chair with the cat basking in its warmth. It
glinted in the gilt-framed mirror above the sideboard, but with an effect very different from
the ghostly light. Not at all the setting one
might expect for an otherworldly visitation.

The rustling of paper drew his attention to his
mother, who sat at the breakfast table, oblivious
to any untoward occurrences. She had arrayed
her stout figure in a morning gown of lavender
muslin, made high at the throat and decorated
with a single knot of ribands. A rather fetching
cap of lace all but hid the long braids of the
graying blond hair—once as burnished a gold
as Tony's—which she wore bound about her
head. She leaned forward, her lorgnette raised
as she concentrated on the contents of the
crossed sheet she held. Fragments of a substantial repast lay on the delicate china plate before
her, and two unopened letters rested near at
hand, awaiting her pleasure.

She was intent on straightening out the life of
another one of her friends, he presumed. They
were forever coming to her with their problems,
in spite of the fact she invariably responded with
volumes of advice. Interrupting her without
compunction, he announced: "Anne was just
here."

Lady Agatha Lambeth looked up, eyebrows
rising in surprise. "That's odd," she said, then
added after a moment: "Did she want breakfast?"

"She flickered out before I could ask."

Lady Agatha nodded. "Probably just checking on you. You came very near to ending the

Lambeth line in that last battle, you know. You must not be surprised if you have her worried."

"She might well be more afraid of our creditors driving her from her home." He leaned back against the windowsill. "Either that, or the place crumbling about her."

His mother regarded him in frowning silence for a long moment. At last, she asked: "Has Bradshaw been able to give you no good news, then?"

"Oh, we'll come about, never fear. It just would have been better if I'd sold out one battle earlier." Only he'd felt it his duty to remain just a little longer, to ride on that blazing June morning with his comrades onto the French-infested field at Vittoria. Well, one couldn't repine. One could only tie knots—no matter how frayed the rope—and move on.

"For the sake of your knee, it certainly would have been better," she agreed, interrupting his thoughts. She set down the letter she'd been reading and eyed him with a frown. "For the estate, it would have made no difference whatsoever."

"I would have been able to ride over the land, see for myself the most urgent needs. And there are so many." He turned back to the window and stared out across the pleasing prospect of scythed lawn and formal gardens that stretched before him beneath the brilliant blue of the late September sky. Beyond lay the lake and a charming Grecian folly. Odd how being grossly encumbered hadn't altered the beauty of the estate—at least near the house. The ruination all lay in the neglected farms.

"At least you only took a ball in your knee," his mother said in the calm, rational voice that had seen him through any number of childhood traumas. "It really would have been too much if you'd gotten yourself killed so soon after—" She stopped herself. "Well, I won't say a word against Reginald. He was my eldest, though I never saw where that bestowed a particle of worth on him. A wastrel, like so many of the Lambeths before him. I can only be grateful for entailments. At least you were able to inherit the estate, even if there isn't a groat with which to set it to rights."

"There is so much I need to see—"

"You can take your curricle almost anywhere you need to go. As for the rest of it, you can rely on our good Bradshaw. He is all that held us together during your father's time, you know. And then Reginald all but broke his heart, allowing the tenanted farms to go to wrack and ruin as he did. Bleeding the land for every penny he could squeeze from it!"

"Had I been here, instead of in the army—" Tony began.

"It would not have made a ha'porth of difference to your brother, and well you know it," his mother interrupted. "You can stop blaming yourself. He wanted money to squander, and squander it he did. Gaming tables and racetracks! And a series of the most elegant and grasping little barques of frailty imaginable."

"Good God!" He stared at her. "He didn't parade them in front of you, did he?"

"He never made any attempt to hide his affairs. No more than his father did."

"But when he married Marianne—"

She made a sound perilously close to a snort. "You never thought there was any love between them, did you? He offered for her because she was the reigning Incomparable. And I do give her that, she is a pretty little widgeon. But she never had a say in the choosing of her husband, her mama made sure of that! Sold her to the only title she could snare."

"Marianne never seemed unhappy," Tony ventured.

"You were not around to see. But one thing is certain, she is not unhappy now, yet she's a widow of barely five months. No, Reginald was too busy wasting money to bother endearing himself to her. He made her a leader of fashion, insisted she squander a fortune on her back, but I'll swear she never enjoyed it."

"Yet she is gone up to London, now."

"At her mama's insistence. I doubt she'll stay for long."

So his sister-in-law would be back soon. That made it imperative he move forward with his intentions now, before she returned to add her dismayed protests to the ones his mother would undoubtedly make. The obligations of honor weighed more with him than even his financial difficulties, though he couldn't expect the two ladies who depended on him to view the matter in a similar light.

Moving stiffly, for his left knee refused to support his weight as it ought, he crossed to the sideboard on which the butler had arranged an inviting array of covered dishes, baskets of pastry, and pitchers of beverages. He selected one of the latter, of chased silver filled with a golden amber liquid, and poured a generous amount of the ale into his tankard. He took a long bracing drink, then leaned back against the heavily carved cabinet. His somber gaze rested once more on his mother.

She met it with a quizzical stare of her own. "You're certainly solemn. Do you have some momentous purpose in mind?"

He cleared his suddenly dry throat and barged ahead. "I thought we might go into Bath this morning."

"And the prospect vexes you?" She tilted her head to one side, her frowning consideration belied by the gleam in her gray eyes. "Do not tell me you intend to drink the waters! I doubt they would do your knee a particle of good."

"Quite the reverse, I should think."

She picked up her teacup and regarded him over the rim. "Then what are you about?"

He forced a lightness into his voice. "I am about to answer your fondest prayers."

"What, have you lured Lady Gresham's cook into leaving her employ?" she demanded, but her gaze narrowed as it rested on his face.

He braced himself with another swallow of ale. "I fear he remains adamant. Will you not settle for my presenting you with a daughter-in-law, instead?"

"A—" Lady Agatha sat very still for a long moment. "How?" she demanded at last. "You have said not one word about being head over heels in love with anyone."

"That need not be a requirement for marriage," he pointed out.

Her cup collided with its saucer with a resounding clatter. "There is no urgency about the matter."

"Is there not? Did you not think our ghostly Anne had taken to checking on me out of fear our line might fail?"

"I wasn't serious. I know you've been made aware of your own mortality, but I assure you—"

"No, listen, love. I have thought this out very carefully. The matter of the succession has been very much on my mind since Reginald died, and I'm determined not to neglect my duty, no matter my personal feelings."

"But if you are not in love—"

His hand clenched the handle of his tankard. "I know your matrimonial ambitions for me, but that was before I was crippled."

"You aren't!" Her eyes flashed. "You are no such thing. I will not have you—"

"I am." The bleakness of his tone cut across her words. "I told you what the doctors have said. I know you dream of me going to London and dancing at balls and losing my heart to some Incomparable—one with a little more sense than Marianne—but that's impossible now. I have no desire to make myself a figure of fun for the entertainment of the *ton*."

"You will never be that," his mama informed him, her voice containing no hint of any inner doubts that might haunt her.

"No, I suppose not" he agreed. "I have a title and estates, so I suppose that qualifies me as a matrimonial prize, even without a fortune, no matter my physical decrepitude. But I have no desire to wed some ambitious little chit who will tolerate me in exchange for becoming Lady Lambeth."

"What utter rubbish! How can you—"

"Easily!" He turned away and limped back to the window. "Do me the courtesy of believing that I have no desire to seek a wife in London."

"You may seek a wife wherever you wish. Only I would not have you make some bloodless marriage of convenience just because you've fallen into a fit of the megrims."

With deliberate steps, he made his way to her and possessed himself of her hands. "Don't fret, love. This isn't a whim born of depression. It's an obvious solution, one that neatly solves both my problems."

"Both?" Her brow snapped down. "Do you mean you intend to offer for some heiress?"

"Good God, no! Have you been listening to Marianne's schemes for me? I only intend to fulfill a promise to Oliver Rycroft."

"Oliver." Her eyes clouded and she squeezed his hands. "The poor boy. At least you could be at his side when he died. But you never told me he made a deathbed request of you."

"Did I not?" Tony kept his voice casual. "It is nothing much, only to look after his sister."

"Calpurnia?" Lady Agatha's brow shot up. "Merciful heavens. You'd need your entire regiment to keep an eye on that little firebrand. Or has she settled a trifle?" She shook her head. "I suppose she's quite grown. I don't believe I've laid eyes on her since they rented out the Gables and moved to town. When was that, four years ago? Yes, for it was when Oliver bought his pair of colors and joined your regiment. Calpurnia's been living with an aunt since her mama died, has she not?"

"So Oliver thought. But it seems she left there to take up a position as a governess almost a year ago."

"A governess! What family in their right mind—" She broke off. "Well, that's neither here nor there. But still, she could be no more than twenty now. That's much too young!"

"So it proved. She seems to have had several employers during the last year, and registered with several agencies, so my man of affairs has had some difficulty tracking her for me. We've finally succeeded, though. She has but recently taken up the position as companion to a Mrs. Bagshott in Bath. Are you acquainted with the lady?"

"Elvina Bagshott?" A choke of laughter escaped Lady Agatha. "Now, there's a pairing! I don't know which I should feel the more sorry for. No, I should actually. Poor Calpurnia, if she's forced to try to please a woman like that. You may count upon it, she will already have been turned off, and very likely without a character. Elvina is the most dreadful woman."

Tony considered for a moment, then nodded to himself. "That makes my decision the best for both of us, then."

A moment of stilled silence followed this pronouncement. Then: "Decision?" his mama asked in a voice of foreboding.

"Certainly. As I said, the solution is obvious. I need a wife who will produce the necessary heir, and who is independent enough not to need me to be forever dancing attendance upon her or taking her to balls. I also need to look after Callie Rycroft, for you must admit she has certainly been reduced to unacceptable straits. This way, I can do both. It's the very thing."

"Is it?" his mama asked in failing accents.

He studied her face and read real distress in her piercing gray eyes. He gave her hands a light shake. "Come now, can you not bear the thought of having Callie as a daughter-in-law? She may take over those chores of organization which you find so distasteful, and for which Marianne proved so completely hopeless. As I remember, she was the most eminently capable little thing. And she'd make an intelligent companion for you, one who wouldn't spout ill-considered nonsense like Marianne does."

"A companion." Lady Agatha grasped at that. "Yes, much better she just be my companion. I shall be only too delighted to hire her. She would never bore me, and she would always have the energy to take on the most difficult tasks. You are quite right, it would be the perfect solution."

"Not your companion, Mama. I shall marry her." He inserted just a hint of steel into the words.

"But there is no need!" Her grip tightened on his fingers. "Truly, there is not."

"Hiring her is hardly looking after her," Tony pointed out.

"But you don't have to *marry* her," Lady Agatha exclaimed. "By next season, you will be so much recovered that you will be longing to return to London. What if you meet someone and fall desperately in love? Don't tie yourself into a marriage of convenience until you have given yourself a chance!"

"Yours was a love match, Mama," he said softly. He let that sink in for a moment, then went on. "Forgive me, but I saw how unhappy my father often made you. I would rather enter into a union with my eyes wide open. I stand a better chance of finding happiness by marrying a childhood friend who is in need of help, than I do tying myself to some unknown chit with a beguiling face."

His mother studied him for a long moment. "The last time I saw Calpurnia was four years ago. She hardly looked to me like one who would make a gentleman a comfortable wife. Has she changed that much?" Her gaze narrowed as he hesitated. "You haven't seen her either, have you?"

His jaw clenched. "I have made my decision. Will you not support me in it?"

She studied his face with ferocity, then made a vexed exclamation and pulled her hands free. "You can be as stubborn and foolish as your father and brother! Very well, I will support you on one condition. We shall invite her here on an extended visit to me, and we may all see how well you like your choice. Let there be no talk of marriage until you have at least seen the girl. Will you settle for that?"

He bent forward and dropped a light kiss on her forehead. "Very well. Until I have seen her. Now, shall I order the carriage?"

   As he started from the room, the ghostly
light flickered once more at the edges of his
vision.

Two

The never-ending parade of people in the Pump Room amused Miss Calpurnia Rycroft. When viewed with a measure of imagination, it could be quite as good as attending the theater, she supposed, though she had never been privileged to attend a performance of a play. If she could not be out and doing something herself, at least here she could sit and observe—and speculate upon—a multitude of little dramas and comedies; and they were all the more fascinating because they would continue, and she could see how they developed from day to day.

Mrs. Elvina Bagshott, her employer of just under six weeks—though most likely not for much longer—gave a loud sniff. "Indecent, I tell you," she informed the elderly Miss Dysart, who sat at her side. "Just look at the gown that chit is wearing. Fast, you mark my words."

Callie turned a considering eye on the garment under discussion, and experienced a twinge of envy. The primrose muslin walking dress would have set off her own soft brown hair to perfection. The rouleaued and flounced skirt swayed with elegant grace, and the hint of lace that filled the deep decolletage struck just the right note. The gentlemen in the room seemed to find nothing at fault with either this creation or the dusky beauty who wore it.

Callie cast a rueful glance at her own serviceable brown merino, made high at the neck and without a single flounce or furbelow. It made her look like some penniless companion—exactly what she was. She'd succeeded admirably at her intention when she'd made it. That knowledge didn't give her as much pleasure as she knew it should.

She turned back to the door in time to see the youthful Captain Ridgeway stroll in, accompanied by two older gentlemen. A charming man; really a dreadful shame he'd lost an arm at Trafalgar. Still, she'd rarely seen anyone who took so much joy in the simple pleasure of just being alive.

More arrivals caused a stir near the entrance, and a straight-backed gorgon entered, followed by a younger gentleman of military bearing but civilian dress. Something about them— Callie straightened, delight bubbling up within her. Tony. Surely, she couldn't be mistaken, not even after so many years. She would know that carefree blond giant anywhere. Memories flooded over her, of his rich, easy laughter, the devilish gleam in his eyes, and that swinging, energetic walk.

At the moment, he neither laughed not walked. For that matter, he didn't look particularly carefree either. He stood still, his frowning gaze sweeping the room.

Callie took a step forward, and realized to

her surprise that she had risen. She had to fight the urge to run to him, as if she were still eight and he the outrageous youth six years her senior who had teased her and laughed at her exploits. Or as if she were sixteen again, newly aware that her childhood idol cut a very heroic figure.

"What are you about, girl?" demanded the petulant voice of Mrs. Bagshott. "Sit down."

"I saw an old friend. I thought I might—"

"You may speak to her later. I need you here."

Callie's eyebrows rose. "Do you wish another glass of the waters, ma'am?"

Mrs. Bagshott's querulous expression turned to one of distaste. "Impudent girl. No one wishes them." With a sniff, she turned back to Miss Dysart, who had risen to take her leave.

Their goodbyes should take several minutes, but now it would be as much as her position was worth to go to Tony. She looked for him, and found he had advanced into the room, still gazing about, probably seeking any acquaintances. With every ounce of her concentration, she willed him to look her way.

The elegant woman at his side touched his arm, and he stooped to hear whatever she said in his ear. His mother, Callie realized, with a delight not unmingled with a sense of trepidation. In those days when she and her brother Oliver had been in and out of the Grange as often as their own home on the neighboring estate, she'd developed a healthy respect for that redoubtable daughter of a marquis.

Tony continued his survey of the room until

he turned to look directly at her. Callie's breath caught in her throat, and it took a struggle to keep her eagerness from showing in her face. For a long moment he studied her, then recognition lit in his eyes and he bent to speak a word in his parent's ear.

So he remembered her. Even after so much time, when she must have grown out of all knowing, he still recognized her. Her spirits lightened, and the burden of sorrow she had carried since her brother's death eased a trifle.

Tony and Lady Agatha started forward. Toward her table, Callie realized. A coincidence? Or could he possibly be pleased to see her, as well? She hardly dared hope. Then she saw him take a halting step, and a soft exclamation broke from her. He limped heavily, and the tense set of his jaw betrayed the pain he struggled to keep in check. She had to force herself not to rise again, not to run to his side to spare him the steps to come to her.

In movement he seemed alien, not at all the athletic, energetic young man she had adored. His broad shoulder jerked with every step as he compensated for the damaged leg. Yet nothing could change his commanding height, and while he'd bulked with muscle as he'd aged, he'd always possessed a strong, well-disciplined body. His dress displayed more of a military cut than she remembered, and his hair had grown a trifle long, falling below his ears, giving him a rakish air that sent the oddest sensation through the pit of her stomach.

He looked up, met her gaze, and the briefest smile lit his eyes. Too brief. That troubled her, even more than did his halting limp. Tony had been—*should be*—a creature of recklessness and fun, of lighthearted humor. The spark of mischievous fun that danced in his eyes had always bound her to him. And now it had gone out, like a flame quenched by the roiling tides of war.

Oliver had drowned in those murky depths, one of so many British soldiers who fell victim to French rifles. Could they be so cruel as to have taken Tony from her, as well?

As Tony and his mother reached the table, Lady Agatha moved ahead. She looked Callie's employer up and down, then managed a genial smile. "Mrs. Bagshott. I believe it has been some time since I have had the pleasure. Calpurnia," she went on, turning toward her new target without giving the first a chance to respond. "I was most distressed to learn about your brother. Lambeth has been searching for you ever since he came home. Now that we have found you, you will come home to the Grange with us for an extended visit."

Callie blinked. "I will?" Lady Agatha's bluntness she knew well. This invitation—and its implied solicitude—took her by surprise.

Mrs. Bagshott stared from one to the other, her expression veering from surprise to indignation. "You will do no such thing, miss," she informed Callie. "I will thank you to remember you are my paid companion, and it does not please me that you should desert me at this time."

"Then I suppose it would be best if she were

no longer your paid companion," declared Lady Agatha.

Callie, whose anger had flared at the selfishness of her employer's words, glanced across at Tony in sudden, appreciative humor. "Your mama doesn't change, does she?"

That brought a fleeting return of the smile she had missed. He stepped forward, neatly eclipsing his forthright parent. "I am sorry if this inconveniences you, Mrs. Bagshott—" he began.

"Inconveniences? Of course it does," she declared. "I have not yet found a replacement for her!"

" 'Not yet'?" Callie straightened, her amusement vanishing. "Do you mean you have already been advertising for one, and you haven't bothered to tell me? You intended to turn me off without notice, with nowhere to turn?"

"You are far too pert, miss," Mrs. Bagshott informed her. "I do not know why I have put up with you this long."

"Possibly because you can find no one else who will cater to your unreasonable demands!" Callie declared before she could stop herself.

"Unreasonable? You call me *unreasonable!* Never have I been so taken in!" Mrs. Bagshott declared in failing accents. "To think I have offered you the sanctuary of my home, cared for you as if you were my own daughter, only to be so brutally betrayed. I cannot bear to look at you a moment longer." She leaned one elbow on the table and lowered her face into her hand.

"Then I shall relieve you of my unwanted

presence!" Callie shot back, her outrage over-coming her. Yet even as the ill-considered words sprang from her mouth, she recognized the un-wisdom of what she did. In a single burst of temper, she not only had severed her source of livelihood, she also had assured that she would be unable to find another. She had to learn to control her unruly tongue—or more impor-tantly, her volatile spirits that led to her unfor-tunate outbursts.

Mrs. Bagshott's head snapped up. "You will do nothing of the sort. Oh!" She slumped in her chair, adopting an enfeeblement at striking odds with her sparkling eyes. "Wicked, unfeel-ing girl. You have brought on my palpitations."

Callie, who had suffered through any num-ber of these displays and found her employer no worse at their conclusion, regarded her with a kindling eye. "Shall I get you a glass of the waters, ma'am?"

Mrs. Bagshott closed her eyes and shud-dered. "To think I have harbored a viper in my bosom," she declared.

"Get her the waters, Callie," Tony said softly. "Leave her to me."

Callie regarded her employer's face, which, far from being pale with imagined illness, had taken on an alarmingly purplish hue. "Oh, I fear she's far beyond that stage," she said with a cheerfulness belied by the bite in her voice. "There's nothing for it but to summon her doc-tor and have a pint or two of blood drawn. Only the other day, I heard one of her friends swear-ing by that as a cure for ill-tempered spleen."

Mrs. Bagshott's eyes flew open. "Get out of

my sight! Dreadful, ungrateful girl! I want you
gone from my home within the hour!"

Callie bobbed her a curtsy. "Of course,
ma'am. I am always eager to do your bid-
ding." With that, she turned and stalked away
from the table.

Partway to the door, she slowed her steps.
Her breath came far too rapidly and hot color
burned in her cheeks. At best, she had just
scandalized half the citizenry of Bath. At worst,
she had assured that she would never again be
able to earn a living. She blinked rapidly to
clear the mist from her eyes, but it kept coming
back with a vengeance.

Someone stopped at her side, and she glanced
up to see Lady Agatha. She looked away quickly.
"My wretched temper," she said with a hollow
laugh. "Pray, forgive me, ma'am. You will probably think better of your invitation to me, and
indeed, I could not blame you."

"On the contrary." Lady Agatha regarded
her with a measure of speculation. "I begin to
feel I may have been wrong. No, pay me no
heed, child. You will come on that visit to us,
as soon as we may retrieve your things from
that dreadful woman's house."

Callie shook her head. "That was not at all
well done of me. I should never have said such
horrid things, but I have borne so much from
that—that *insufferable* woman! And then to
learn she intended to treat me so shabbily! It
was the final straw. But there was no excuse for
such ill-bred behavior, and I am so very sorry
you had to witness it."

"Nonsense." Lady Agatha patted her shoulder. "I haven't been so entertained this age. And here comes Lambeth to join us."

Tony strolled up in a manner designed to disguise his limp, but which failed miserably. "Speaking of people who haven't changed," he said, shaking his head. "You sounded exactly as you did ten years ago, when you were rattling me off in prime style for some prank I'd pulled on you."

"You see what I'm up against?" Callie said with a shaky smile. "I try to control my tongue— and my temper. Really, I do. In fact, this is the first time they've cost me a position. Before, it's been because I've been too young, or some silly young fish-face with spots has tried to make up to me, or—oh, any number of the most ridiculous reasons!"

An unfamiliar seriousness shone in Tony's eyes. "Clearly, you were never cut out to be a governess or companion."

"You underestimate Calpurnia," his mother informed him. "I believe she has the resolution of spirit to do anything to which she sets her mind."

Tony opened his mouth, met his mother's steady gaze, and closed it again. "So did Mrs. Bagshott underestimate her," he said after a moment.

Impulsively, Callie clasped Lady Agatha's hand. "Indeed, ma'am, you can have no idea how grateful I am to you. To both of you," she corrected quickly. "I could not have borne with that insufferable woman for many more days, but you must know I have been at my wit's end, for try as I might, I have been unable to discover another position. And now I must impose on an old friendship by taking you up on your kind offer, for I greatly fear I have burned my last bridge."

Callie stood in the center of the sunny bedroom to which Mrs. Durstan, the Lambeths' housekeeper, had shown her, and looked around, frowning. Already, she regretted the unfortunate need to accept this generous hospitality. She hadn't known such luxury since her mother had been forced to rent out, and then sell, their own home, the Gables. She cut off thoughts of those spacious, cheerful rooms, so well remembered and loved. They were a far cry from her aunt's town house in a less than fashionable quarter of London. And as for the succession of rooms it had been her dubious pleasure to occupy during the months of her employment! She shuddered at the recollection of accommodations that had ranged from cramped rooms on the damp north sides of houses, to a cubbyhole in the servants' quarters. If she weren't careful, she would renew her taste for the elegant and luxurious here at Lambeth Grange. That was something, in her position, she could not afford to do.

Yet here she stood in a chamber flooded with warmth and light; the golden rays danced off the yellows and creams of the fabrics and wallpaper. A giant vase of pink and white roses stood on the dresser, and a welcoming fire crackled in the hearth, dispelling the last traces of stuffiness from a room she doubted had been used in the six years since the death of Tony's father. And not so much as a whiff of the tallow or mildew to which she had grown inured.

Lady Agatha paused just inside the doorway, regarding her visitor with a smile that held considerable speculation. To Callie, Tony's parent had always seemed such a remote figure, unapproachable; now she returned the steady regard with interest. Lady Agatha looked older, of course, with more gray in her fading blond hair. Yet her eyes were every bit as bright as they had ever been, gleaming with intelligence and—

And something more. Lady Agatha Lambeth had some purpose in mind, and it involved Callie.

"What is it?" Callie asked, ever blunt.

Lady Agatha considered her a moment longer, then seemed to come to some decision. "How does my son strike you?" she asked.

Callie frowned. "He has changed, of course. But in the course of four years, that is hardly remarkable. The war has certainly left its mark on him. But I haven't spoken to him yet. *Really* spoken to him, I mean. He barely uttered a word in the carriage. What exactly is it you wish me to do?"

At that, Lady Agatha's mouth twitched into a smile. "You are not one to mince words, Calpurnia, I'll grant you that. I want you to help me rid him of this nonsensical notion that he has nothing left in life to which he may look forward."

"Was that your purpose in bringing me here?"

Lady Agatha hesitated. "He has a purpose of his own, but I will allow him to tell you of that. Suffice it to say that I rely on your judgment to assure he will do nothing which he may regret."

Callie blinked at her, alarm rising. "Good heavens, ma'am, have you reason to fear he may do something rash? Put a period to his existence, perhaps? I cannot think of anything less like Tony—at least, like the Tony I knew."

"No! No, I thank God for that. But there are other, also irrevocable, mistakes he may make while in the depths of despair. I simply do not want him to commit to anything that he may wish undone when he has had a chance to heal."

"I see. No, to be honest, I don't see. But I suppose I shall, once he has explained this mysterious purpose to me. I promise I will do what I can to bring him out of this fit of the dismals."

"Thank you. I rely on you, my dear." She held Callie's gaze a moment. "Well, I hope you will be comfortable in here."

Callie cast a rueful glance about the generous proportions and elegant furnishings of her quarters. "You will spoil me. It will be quite your own fault if I refuse to move out when the time comes."

A startled, apprehensive look entered her hostess's eyes, but all she said was: "Nonsense."

Heavy footsteps approached down the hall, and two footmen entered, each carrying a bandbox. One managed a small valise as well.

These they deposited on chairs, then took themselves off.

"You will want to settle in before dinner," Lady Agatha said. "I will leave you for now. We will meet in the Blue Salon at six." With that, she exited.

Callie regarded the closing door with a puzzled frown. It offered no answers; she would have to seek out Tony and demand explanations as to what his mother was about. But first she would have to unpack and make herself more presentable in deference to her present august surroundings.

A tap sounded on the door, and before Callie could open it a maid entered, a girl not much older than Callie herself, with the fresh complexion of country living. She bobbed a shy curtsy. "If you please, miss, I'm Jenny, and I'll be serving as lady's maid for you."

Callie shook her head. "There's not the least need."

The girl's eyes widened. "Of course there is, miss." She crossed to the meager luggage and opened the nearest of the bandboxes. "Now, you'll be needing one of your dresses pressed before dinner, I shouldn't doubt." She pulled out two simple round gowns of serviceable merino, one brown and the other dove gray. A third, of gray muslin, followed. With a frown, Jenny reached for the other bandbox.

"They'll be sadly creased," Callie warned. "They've been packed away for more than a year."

"Don't worry, miss. I'll do one now, then

the others when there's time to see to them proper."

She opened the case that had traveled with Callie throughout her various positions. From it Jenny drew three silver-wrapped gowns, Callie's favorites with which she had not been able to bear to part. A figured muslin morning dress the maid laid aside, followed by a deep green riding habit. The last, an amber crepe open robe over a sarcenet underdress, the maid brought forth with a soft exclamation of triumph.

This she laid across the bed, then turned her attention to removing the meager collection of petticoats, stays, nightdresses, stockings, handkerchiefs, and all the other accoutrements to a companion's wardrobe, and bestowing them in the capacious wardrobe. The gowns went in next, and the brush, comb, and hairpins found new homes on the dresser.

At last, she draped the evening gown over her arm. "If you'll excuse me, I'll just see to this. Albert—he's one of the footmen, miss—he'll be along shortly to take away your bags." With that, she bobbed another curtsy and exited.

Callie watched her go, not at all sure she liked this abrupt change in her circumstances. Recent years had accustomed her to looking after herself. She could cut and sew her own gowns as well as any seamstress, wield an iron with the prowess of an experienced laundry maid, and style her own or her employer's hair with the precision of a top-lofty dresser. In short, she had almost become resigned to per-

forming the innumerable tasks which normally
fell under the province of an abigail. To be on
the receiving end of such services once again
would be a luxury. She must try not to let this
interlude spoil her for the life to which she
must shortly return.

A sudden chill sent a shiver up her spine,
and the hairs on the nape of her neck stood
on end. An eerie feeling she couldn't shake
took possession of her. She looked around, but
could see no one. She was alone, except for
the fire. She shivered again, and went to stand
in the warmth of the sunlight that spilled
through the window.

That helped. She looked out across the impressive view that met her gaze, of the rolling
scythed lawn at the back of the house, an ancient and impressive rose garden, and a shrubbery maze of impressive proportions. She
remembered the latter well; it had been a favorite place to play when they'd been children. From this room, she could almost—but
not quite—make out the paths that would
lead to the center. There'd been a fountain
and benches and several statues, as she recalled.

It seemed impossible to believe she was really
back. Almost she could see her brother racing
across the lawn in laughing pursuit of Tony,
then the two turning to wave to her before darting on, leaving her to follow as best she could,
vexed by her hampering narrow skirts and
dainty slippers. Most of the time, she'd caught
them up. Other times she'd been distracted
into following a pheasant or other wild crea-

ture, until she'd wound up beside the stream
where she tossed in pebbles or twigs until they
came searching for her, fearing her lost.

Resolutely, she dragged her thoughts from
the past. Oliver was gone, and Tony— She had
a job to do, there. And the sooner she set about
it, the better all would be. She might as well
begin by finding out what mysterious purpose
he had in mind for her.

As she reached the foot of the great oak staircase, she hesitated, unsure in which apartment
her host might be found. A brief search turned
up no results in either the morning room or
the Gold Salon, but as she headed toward the
conservatory at the back of the house, Tony
emerged with his halting gait from the library.

"There you are!" She strode up to him at
once. "I was wondering where you might have
gotten to. I want to have a word with you."

"You do?" The harsh lines of pain eased in
his face. "Excellent. I wish to have a few with
you, as well. Will you not come into the library?" He took her arm and led her into the
room from which he'd just emerged.

She entered the large apartment with considerable curiosity. This had not been one of the
rooms where the children had been encouraged to run tame, being the sanctuary of Tony's
father. The comforting scents of old leather,
lemon oil, and beeswax greeted her. It seemed
a vast, open space, lined with cases crammed
with books everywhere except for the doors on
either end of the long room and the French
window opposite her, which led out to the terrace. A sofa, several chairs, and a low table

stood in the center before the massive hearth, and someone had arranged another grouping of chairs and tables at one end of the room. A black and white cat slept in one of these. At the other end of the room stood a massive cherrywood desk with several chairs placed about it. Tony led her toward these, and seated her with such punctilious politeness that a sense of foreboding started deep within her.

He half sat against the edge of his desk, his frowning gaze resting on her. "It's been an age since we have seen one another," he said after a moment. "So much has happened."

"Yes." She studied the unwarranted seriousness of his expression. "I was sorry to hear about Reginald."

"You'll be even more sorry when you see the straits to which he has reduced the farms," he said, then added abruptly: "You got my letter about Oliver."

She looked up and saw in his eyes a mirrored reflection of her own grief. "I am glad of the opportunity to thank you for that. You were always such a good friend to him. It gave me great comfort to know you were with him at—at the end."

His jaw tensed. "It gave me comfort, as well. And that," he added with an attempt at a lighter tone, "is, in part, why I've brought you here."

He hesitated, and Callie looked up to meet his eyes. They'd changed. The lines of laughter that had crinkled the corners remained, but they held tension now. In the dark gray depths she saw pain and sorrow, not the deviltry that had so delighted her throughout her youth. "Ah," she said, nodding wisely. "Now we come to it. Your mama said you had some fell purpose."

"Did she?" He cast her a sharp glance. "Did she tell you what it is?"

"No. She insisted that you be the one. Do you know, Tony, everything has happened so quickly, and I was in such a temper before, I do not believe I have had the chance to say how delightful it is to see you again. It quite takes one back."

A sudden, boyish grin transformed his features. "It does, does it not?" The next moment the grin faded beneath the more recent lines of strain. "But there is no going back. One may only go on, and try to make the best of what one can find." He paused a moment, staring off into space. Without looking at her, he said: "We have known one another for most of our lives, have we not?"

"Of a certainty. Though I cannot remember which of us led the others into the most scrapes."

A reminiscent gleam lit his tired eyes. "You were always the most shocking hoyden. So very capable."

"Well, if you mean I was always able to tell a convincing story to cover our exploits, I suppose so."

He frowned down into her upturned face. "What I remember is an eager, energetic child who would not be easily intimidated and could look after herself very well, who had little need of aid from either Oliver or me."

"What on earth is this about, Tony? You sound so formal. I know we have not seen one another this age, but truly, four years is not so great a time."

"Forgive me, but you've grown up. You might have changed, but you seem very much the same. No, I'm wrong. You've developed more poise, more surety. That's good."

"Is it?" She tilted her head to one side, considering him. "Look, do you want me to do something for you, but you don't know how to ask? Is that it? Is your mama fagging you to death about your injuries? I'll try to speak to her about it if you wish, though I doubt she'll pay me any heed."

For a long moment, he didn't answer. Then: "Tell me, do you enjoy being a companion?"

She blinked at this abrupt change in subject. "It is far more congenial than being a governess," she assured him after a moment.

His lips twitched. "Which is to say you find it somewhat preferable to becoming a prize-fighter or treading the boards?"

"Somewhat," she agreed.

"And you have parted—rather irrevocably, I fear—with your current employer."

She shuddered. "Pray, do not remind me. I am mortified, I promise you. But to what purpose are you leading me?" She brightened. "Do you perhaps know of someone in search of an impoverished young lady of willing disposition? That's the way the advertisements usually read, you know."

"As a matter of fact, that description suits

rather well. But I'm not looking for a companion, but a wife.''

"A—" She stared at him, completely taken aback.

He swore softly and rose. "Forgive me. I'm making a mull of this. But I haven't much experience in offering for someone.''

"Tony—"

He turned back to her. "You can't tell me you don't think we should suit, Callie. We've known one another too well for that.''

"But—"

"And I can be far more congenial than your Mrs. Bagshott. I would be glad of your lively company for my mother, as well as for my sister-in-law. And as for myself—" Again, his jaw set. "To be blunt, I need an heir. I know I'm no great catch with this"—he gestured toward his leg—"but I hoped that because of our long friendship you might be willing to accept me.''

A companion for his mother? An heir for himself? Her indignation, only so recently cooled from her morning's outburst, flared once more. "I see. And how did you happen to hit upon me as a likely choice for this honor?''

If he heard the sarcasm in her voice, he ignored it. "Oliver asked me to look after you—"

"Oh, he did, did he?'' she muttered.

"—of which I've done a deplorable job since my return. And since I must have a bride, and I have no desire to seek one in London, this seemed the obvious and sensible solution.''

"Obvious and sensible." She directed a falsely sweet smile at him. "Let me understand you. You wish to marry me for the sole purpose of fulfilling a promise to my brother?"

He regarded her with a puzzled frown. "That, and the other reasons I gave you."

"To be sure. How forgetful of me. Oliver wrote me how your brother played at ducks and drakes with the Lambeth fortune. But do you truly think that marrying me will be less costly than hiring me as a companion for your mother?"

"Lord, you're not going to be missish, are you, Callie? I hadn't thought it of you." Abruptly, his face clouded. "Or is it that you cannot bear the thought of being leg-shackled to a wreck of a man?"

She closed her eyes, tried to force her soaring temper under control, and failed miserably. "What I cannot bear," she said through gritted teeth, "is to be married because you happen to find it a convenient solution to your momentary problems! Where will that leave us in a year's time, when you have recovered much of the use of your leg and your mama has had her fill of my acid tongue?" She surged to her feet. "You may take your obliging proposal, *my lord*, and go to the devil with it!"

Three

Cheeks burning with her wrath, Callie stormed into the hall. From behind her came Tony's voice, calling for her to wait. The sound of his uneven steps penetrated her anger; he would pursue her, and it would not be good for him. Reluctantly she stopped and turned back.

"Dash it, Callie, you have the devil's own temper!" he declared as he caught her up.

"You should have remembered that before you offered for me. Just see what a narrow escape you have had."

"I'm beginning to think you may be right!" He glared at her; then a sudden, rueful light lit in his eyes. "I don't know what I could have said, though, that made you as mad as a wet hen."

"Oh, you don't, don't you? You offer me an insult like that, and you think it should please me, perhaps?"

"An insult? Good God. How did I do that? I *offered* for you, for heaven's sake. Now, if it had been a different sort of arrangement—" He broke off, and a dull flush crept up from his neck. "Lord, who am I to talk about unruly tongues? Sorry, Callie."

She stared at him, then burst out laughing, mostly in sheer exasperation. "You are an idiot!" she informed him when she could speak again. "And odious, into the bargain. Oh, Tony, how on earth could you have proposed to me in terms such as those?"

His expression remained puzzled. "I'll admit I'm no great hand at the matter, but I thought I laid out the situation clearly. Is it not a compliment that, when I sought a wife, I thought first of you?"

She started to speak, but as his words sank in, she broke off, shaken. Viewed in that light, she supposed it was a compliment. But he sought her for all the wrong reasons. Why, precisely, friendship and a desire for mutual benefit were the wrong ones, and what would be the right ones from him, she didn't choose to explore at the moment.

"Come," he said. "I thought we were too good friends for me to insult you when I intended rather to show my appreciation of you. Have I mistaken the matter?"

She drew a deep ragged breath. "No. Of course we are friends."

"That's an excellent basis for marriage," he pointed out. "Shall we not make a match of it?"

She folded her arms, hugging herself. "You can do better than some penniless Nobody, Tony. And I cannot believe this has your mama's approval."

A deep crease formed in his brow. "She desires to see me wed."

"Of a certainty. But to some lady of fashion—and fortune."

"She doesn't see what I've become."

Her mouth pursed. "Or are you merely making too much of it?"

"I've made up my mind." His jaw tensed, then relaxed with a visible effort. "Come, Callie, it's the simplest solution to both our problems."

"Simplest, possibly." But was it the best for him? He'd always been one for making logical decisions without due reflection on the emotional aspects. Some he'd even come to regret later.

This one, she suspected, would shortly become one of his regrets.

But his mind, as he'd said, was made up. And his was a mind almost as stubborn as hers.

"If you have something better waiting for you in the offing, please feel free to tell me," he invited.

She directed a disdainful look at him, but his words set her mind racing. Her future, as she would be the first to admit, looked pretty bleak. Marriage to Tony—for whatever reason—was certainly better than anything she ever could have hoped for. But she could not bring herself to marry where she did not love, and was not loved in return.

He said nothing more, just stood there watching her. Quite openly, she studied his face, searching the familiar planes and angles, the unfamiliar lines. And his eyes. They didn't sparkle. Instead, they held a sea of troubles, a wealth of self-loathing. Merciful heavens, she reflected soberly, had she added more torment to his already overburdened estimation of himself? What would it do to him if she—the one female to whom he trusted his shaken self-worth—rejected him?

Lady Agatha's words sprang to mind, and repeated themselves over and over. Don't let him do something he would regret. Had his mother referred to this marriage that Tony proposed? Or did she fear that if Callie turned him down, he would turn in desperation to another, highly unsuitable, female to salvage his pride? There had to be some solution, some compromise.

Abruptly, she said: "May we go out to the terrace? I feel the need of a breath of fresh air."

"Of course." He offered her his arm.

She laid her fingers on his sleeve. Through the soft cloth, she could feel his muscles tense with the effort of his movement. She pretended to ignore it. He would hardly appreciate her being aware of any weakness on his part, especially now that she had already wounded him.

They left the house through the library, letting themselves out onto the terrace where they walked to the balustrade. Tony seemed lost in his own thoughts, which gave her the opportunity to subject him to a more thorough, covert study. Gone, she realized sadly, was the hero of her childhood; she could detect no traces of the adventurous youth she had adored. That caused her pain, to see him so much changed, so convinced of his lack of worth.

She could not add to that. He would recover, of course, but it would take time. Well, she could give him that time. A mock betrothal—at least on her side—would set him up once more in his self-conceit. Then, when his spirits and health were restored sufficiently for him to regret his offer, she would release him from his promises.

She considered the plan, and found it acceptable. She could be of real service to him—earn her keep, in some small way. And it had the added advantage of allowing her a respite from her search for further employment.

She drew a steadying breath. "Tony? Am I permitted to change my mind?"

He looked down at her. "Of a certainty. It is a trifle chilly out here. You should have brought a shawl."

She burst out laughing. "Not that, you idiot. About marrying you. If you have not thought better of your offer, I think I should like to become engaged to you, after all."

His gaze narrowed. "Engaged. You worded that very carefully, did you not?"

She leaned her elbows on the railing and stared out across the lawn. "I did, rather, didn't I? But I refuse to take advantage of you when you are despondent."

"You have been talking to my mama! Callie—"

"No." She stopped him with a fierce look. "Have you ever known me to be influenced by another before?"

His indignation wavered into sudden, reminiscent amusement. "Lord, when I think of the times Oliver and I tried to dissuade you from some freakish start—" He shook his head.

"There, you see? I am quite capable of making my own decisions. You have done me the honor of informing me that you only wish to marry me because you have no desire to be troubled with looking elsewhere for a wife." She held up her hand to stop his embarrassed protest. "I know I must be the oddest of creatures, but I cannot rid myself of the fear that once you have somewhat recovered from your injury, you will regret the engagement. Indulge me in this, please. If you have not succumbed to the desire to be free of me by the beginning of the Season, I will marry you." And she would have to trust in his powers of recovery to make that unnecessary.

"And if you decide you cannot go through with it?"

She tossed him a saucy smile as she turned away. "Well, it will be up to you to see that I don't, won't it?"

"Minx" He caught up to her. "Come back to the library. I've got something for you."

Her eyebrows rose, but she accompanied him. The sudden darkness after the bright sunlight outdoors nearly blinded her as they stepped through the French windows, and by the time she could see again, he had passed her and approached the massive desk. He circled to its far side, opened the top drawer, and removed a small box. A jeweler's box, she realized as she joined him. He raised the lid, drew out a ring, and turned back to her. A large sapphire stone, with six broad facets, glinted in a delicate gold setting.

Taking her hand, he slipped it onto her finger. "An engagement present. It has been in my family for generations."

She shivered and pulled back her hand. "It's cold!"

"I suppose I should have had a fire lit in here. Don't worry, it will warm soon enough on your finger."

"It's prickling, too." She regarded it with a frown. "Why—" She broke off as a light knock sounded on the door, and it opened.

Durstan, the butler who had served at Lambeth Grange for as long as Callie could remember, stepped over the threshold. His long, hollowed face remained devoid of expression, but the vibrancy of his voice belied the frailty of his build as he announced: "Mr. Felix has arrived, m'lord."

"Felix?" Tony straightened. "Good God. What the devil is he doing here?"

"I really couldn't say, m'lord. You will have to see him for yourself," came the candid response. With that, the ancient servitor turned on his heel and exited.

A choke of laughter escaped Callie. "I don't remember him being that impertinent!" she declared.

A sheepish grin replaced Tony's frown. "What can I do? He's known me since I was in the cradle. And he was always one to show me a kindness when I'd fallen into some scrape or other. And frequently because of you and Oliver."

"I remember him smuggling some sweetmeats up to me on the night of your mama's ball. I could have been no more than twelve, but they'd allowed me to come and watch, do you remember? Only they banished me to the nursery for—heavens, Tony, I cannot recall."

"Something outrageous, I make no doubt." He dropped the jewelry box back into the drawer. "Shall we go and see why the deplorable Felix has chosen to honor us with a visit?"

"I haven't seen him in ages. Has he changed?" In a much lighter mood, she accompanied him toward the Great Hall.

"Felix? Change?" Tony shook his head. "Never."

From ahead of them, a light, merry voice rose in an effusive greeting. "My dear Cousin Agatha! Seeing you is enough to make me almost glad I was driven to visit Bath."

They entered the hall to see Felix Lambeth, the young cousin of Tony's late father, bending over Lady Agatha's hand and kissing her fingers with practiced flair. He was resplendent in a coat of Bath cloth, an elegant neckcloth, and a waistcoat that boasted so vivid a design and hue as to command instant attention. Tony came to an abrupt halt, groped for his quizzing glass, and leveled it on the outrageous garment. "So it's finally happened," he said sadly, shaking his head.

That caused his erratic relative pause. "What has?" Felix demanded, rife with suspicion.

"Too many nights staring at green baize cloths. You've lost your ability to see colors."

"Military men." Felix shook his head sadly. "Not the least sense of fashion. I'll have you know, this waistcoat is all the crack! I assure you."

"In London, perhaps, but not here."

At that, Felix shuddered. "No need to tell me that, dear coz. Never has it been my fate to sojourn in so boring a spot as Bath." His gaze moved past him and settled on Callie. Instantly he straightened, the image of a dandy. "But you must introduce me to this charming young lady."

"No need. I admit she's grown a trifle, but believe me, in every other respect it's easy to recognize Callie Rycroft."

"*Callie?*" Felix stared at her, openmouthed. "Good God. You've turned into a little beauty! But that gown." He shook his head at her brown merino. "I always thought you was a knowing one when it came to fashion."

"She has more sense than to peacock about in a getup like yours," Tony informed him ruthlessly. "What brings you here?"

"Staying with a friend in Bath. You remember Archibald Trent? Buck teeth and no chin, but the devil with the dice? Had to pop over to visit his godmama, so he begged me to bear him company."

Tony tapped his quizzing glass into the palm of one hand. "As I remember, you swore it would take an act of God to drag you to such a—now, what did you call Bath? Ah, yes. Such a benighted den of dreariness."

"It was. Couldn't have been anything else causing such a curst run of ill luck. Dice devilish against me, dear boy. Nothing for it but to rusticate. And you have to admit, Bath is the one place I could be certain of *not* finding any pleasures. And as for the waters!" He shuddered. "Don't, dear coz, let any of the doctors talk you into trying a cure of them. I made the terrible mistake of letting Archie talk me into taking a sip."

"Which means he lost a bet, and had to drink them as a forfeit," Tony explained in an aside to Callie.

Felix directed a pained look at him, but otherwise ignored the interruption. "Take my advice and stick to that French wine your father laid down. Much more potable."

"Infinitely so, I should think," Tony agreed.

"Felix." Lady Agatha, who had been regarding her late husband's relative in silent contemplation, seemed to come to a decision, and a gleam lit her piercing eye. "You are the very person we want."

"You *want*?" Felix's eyes widened in surprise. "You sure you've got that right? No wish to disillusion you, you know, but I've never been much good to anyone."

"Least of all yourself," she informed him. "You're a wastrel and a reprobate, but you can be charming when you put your mind to it. You will offer your apologies to Mr. Archibald Trent and come and stay here for a few weeks."

"Why?" He eyed her with distinct mistrust. "Now, not that I'm loath to visit the old ancestral hovel, mind you, not when I remember the kegs with which my cousins stocked the cellars. But I can't imagine why you'd be wanting me."

"Neither can I," murmured Tony.

A wicked gleam lit his mama's eyes. "We are forming a house party. Calpurnia has already done us the honor of accepting my invitation."

Felix beamed at Callie, but a slight frown remained to mar his brow. "That is certainly an inducement of no mean order. I should be delighted to renew my acquaintance with her." He rocked back on his heels and, after a moment, added: "I understand Lady Lambeth is currently in London."

"She has been gone less than a se'nnight," Tony confirmed.

"Ah." A fine line eased from Felix's countenance. "Then she is not like to return soon. So you wish to increase your numbers."

"Have you any pressing engagements?" Lady Agatha demanded of him.

"In Bath?" His lip curled in comical disdain. "None that cannot be canceled with a note."

"Then do so, at once. And when that is completed," she added as one experienced in the fine art of bribery, "we may settle down for a comfortable coze over a glass of my late husband's excellent sherry before dinner."

"Dinner," Felix repeated in a thoughtful tone. "Do you still have that chef? French fellow? Second only to Lady Gresham's? Can't recall his name at the moment."

"Armand," supplied Tony.

A beatific smile spread over Felix's face. "We will be dining at six, I suppose? In general, a most uncivilized hour. But when it comes to Armand, I must admit, it seems a pity to wait a moment longer than necessary before sampling his offerings. And now, if you will excuse me for just a few moments? I must send a message to Archie to have my trappings sent out. Oh, and perhaps your groom will return my mount? I only meant to borrow him for the afternoon." With that, he took himself off.

"Whatever possessed you to invite him?" Tony demanded in an undervoice as soon as their relative was out of earshot.

His mother returned his accusing stare with one of intense satisfaction—and a shade too much innocence. "Why, to assure Calpurnia of a convivial house party, of course. You must admit, he adds a certain liveliness to any gathering he graces."

"He adds a great many things," agreed Tony dryly. "And not all of them welcome. What are you about?"

"Just what I said. Now, I must warn our good Mrs. Durstan to have a room prepared."

Callie watched Lady Agatha as she headed off on her errand. "It will seem almost like old times, with Felix here. If only—" She broke off. If only Oliver and Reginald could be there, as well. But voicing the thought only made the desire more real, more difficult to bear. She turned from Tony. "If you will excuse me? There are a few things I should see to."

Leaving Tony frowning after her in the hall, she made her way up the stairs toward her room, her one haven in this house. She had a great deal to consider. For one, Tony's proposal had come as an unwelcome shock to her. The fury of her reaction to it had surprised her even more. And then there had been her conditional acceptance.

The maid Jenny had not yet returned with her pressed gown, she was glad to see. She sank onto the edge of the bed, drew her feet up beneath her, and frowned into space. If she were to take a rational view of the matter, his proposal had been a compliment in its way, just as he said. So why didn't she take the logical view of it? She had long ago outgrown her silly calf love for him. Yet the fact remained that the cool logic of his proposal had infuriated her.

Her hands clenched, and the odd sensation of a ring on one of her fingers claimed her attention. It hadn't warmed to her as Tony had predicted; if anything, its coldness had increased. In fact, it grew uncomfortable.

She turned her hand to examine it more closely. It bore every outward appearance of normality; yet with every passing moment, it gained more and more resemblance to a band of ice. And that wasn't all. It prickled with a persistence that defied explanation. She twisted it, trying to ease the growing itch, but it only seemed to intensify the sensations. Tugging at it did no good, either; it refused to come off, as if it attached itself to her flesh.

The fine hairs rose along the nape of her neck, and she shivered with the chill that had descended on the sunlit chamber.

The ring wouldn't come off.

She studied it, and the glowing stone beckoned her gaze, drawing her into the faceted depths. A flame seemed to dance in the very center, hazy, not quite there. A ghost flame, she thought, and that fanciful description surprised her. She was not, as a general rule, of a fanciful turn of mind. The flickering movement fascinated her as the late afternoon sun that slanted through the window set the flame dancing.

"No, never had the pleasure. Mind, I haven't been that anxious to make her acquaintance, but—"

"*Her?*" Callie interrupted. "Do you mean there really is a ghost here?"

Tony met his mother's startled look. "Was it a flame?" he asked Callie.

She stared at him, openmouthed, in kindling indignation. "You *knew?*" she managed after a moment. "You actually knew, all of you, and you never thought to mention the fact to me?"

"It's Anne Lambeth," Tony told her. "And I did mention her to you, several times. As I remember," he added thoughtfully, "you always told me to quit talking such fustian."

"You were going on about a headless nun charging down the Grand Stair on a ghostly white horse!" she protested. "And you know perfectly well you were only trying to see how much you could make me swallow. Which," she added with righteous vigor, "I never did."

"No, the nun was—" He broke off, frowning in an effort of memory. "Well, I can't recall what I called her. But I'm pretty sure I told you about Anne. Yes, by Jove, I did. She was the one I said had a habit of erupting into flames in the middle of the dining room and then flinging herself out the tower window to try to quench the fires in the lake."

"Tony!" His mother regarded him with disapprobation. "How dare you make fun of poor Anne like that."

"She would have missed the lake by more than a hundred yards," Callie pointed out.

"Well, I didn't properly remember her story," Tony admitted.

Callie, glowering at him, shook her head. "I still can't believe one of your idiotish tales actually contained a grain of truth."

"Several, I think. She does appear as a flame, and she did throw herself from the tower. Didn't she?" he added, turning to his mother for confirmation.

"She did," agreed Lady Agatha. "And I know she's been very active of late, but this is the first time she has ever appeared to someone who is not a member of the family."

Felix, who had been listening in unaccustomed silence, stared from one to the other of them. "I feel slighted! When I think how nearly I'm related, and of all the times I've stayed under this roof, and not once has she shown so much as a flicker! And Callie is in the house for what, no more than a few hours, and Anne has already welcomed her!"

"It does seem rather unusual," agreed Tony.

"Welcoming the prospective bride?" Felix suggested.

Tony shook his head. "She's never paid Marianne a visit. For which Marianne is excessively grateful, I might add. Where were you, Callie?"

"In my room. I was looking at the ring"—she held up her hand, on which she had replaced the circlet of gold with its stone—"and I saw a flame inside it."

"*Inside* it?" Tony took her hand, studied the ring, then led her toward the window.

"There's nothing there, now." She pulled

free, then turned her fingers so the rays flashed off the stone. "See?"

He recaptured her hand and studied the ring with frowning intensity. The contact annoyed her, causing her to breathe more shallowly, and making her vividly aware of him as he towered over her. How dare he stand there, so totally oblivious of everything about her except that ring— Well, she told herself savagely, it was just as well. He had ceased to be her hero years ago, and she had no interest whatsoever in bringing this sham engagement to fruition. He could be as oblivious of her as he chose. And the tingling wave caused by the warmth of his touch only irritated her further.

"It's been locked away in the vault room for some time," he said thoughtfully. "Mama, do you remember ever wearing it?"

"No. It was a favorite of your grandmama's, though."

"By Jupiter, so it was," exclaimed Felix. "I remember that sapphire. There's a necklet and brooch to match, isn't there?"

"And you are certain the flame was in the ring?" Tony pursued, turning back to Callie.

"Of course I am. It flickered inside of it, then it came out, hovered in front of me, then shifted into a hazy figure. And she beckoned to me."

Tony's grip on her hand tightened. "Good God. I've never seen her as more than a flame. Have you?" He looked toward his mother.

"No." Lady Agatha regarded Callie in frowning intensity. "I've never heard of such a thing."

"I daresay I made the whole thing up," offered Callie.

Tony cast her an exasperated glance, but otherwise ignored her comment. "I don't know much of the history of this ring and the other pieces of the set, beyond the fact my grandfather gave them to my grandmother as an engagement gift. Do you know?" he asked his parent.

A crease formed in Lady Agatha's brow. "They were Anne's."

"Anne?" Felix brightened. "Well, well, well. I'll wager that explains it."

Lady Agatha fixed him with a withering look. "You'd wager on anything."

"My only accomplishment." Felix hung his head in pretended shame, but laughter lit his eyes.

"Who was she?" asked Callie, cutting back to the chase. She looked from one to the other of them. "And whatever possessed her to throw herself from the tower?"

"You must know the story best," Tony said, deferring to his mother.

Lady Agatha sank onto a chair near the hearth, in which a comfortable fire blazed. Only the slightest aroma of smoke reached Callie as she settled on the facing sofa. The light had grown dim, she realized with a renewed touch of humor: the perfect time for a ghost tale.

Tony, though, didn't seem to share this romantic view. From a drawer he pulled out a tinderbox and set about lighting a branch of candles.

"Anne Lambeth," Lady Agatha said slowly, "was a devoted Jacobite. She killed herself in 1714."

"Quite the scandal, as I remember the tale," Felix stuck in. "Such a rare to-do. A real beauty, she was. And, if rumors were true, quite a—" He broke off under the quelling effect of Lady Agatha's glare. "Oh, all right. Mum's the word on that. You tell the story."

"Thank you." She eyed her late husband's reprobate relative for a moment longer, but he made no attempt to speak again, so she continued. "She was the daughter of Percival Lambeth and his second wife, Letitia Pennicott. Letitia had a considerable fortune in her own right, and left it all to Anne. Anne's half brother, who was the son of Percival's first wife, didn't hold with the political views of his mama-in-law's family. The Pennicotts supported the Stuarts, you must know, and when Elector George became king here, they gave considerable money to the Old Pretender in France.

"And that," she went on, "was poor Anne's tragedy. She became secretly engaged to Henry Rycroft—yes, a member of your family, Calpurnia. According to the story, she gave her entire fortune into his keeping, believing he would deliver both it and the Rycroft family's fortune to the Jacobite cause. But on the night they intended to elope together, Henry vanished along with both fortunes."

"Well, that wasn't well done of him!" Callie exclaimed. "Betraying both Anne and her cause—" she broke off. "Not the sort of thing one likes to hear about an ancestor, I must say.

I knew there was some scandal in the past, but no one would ever talk about it."

"I'm not surprised." Lady Agatha nodded. "Your family never recovered financially."

Callie glowered at the fire. "It was bad enough, betraying his own family. But poor Anne. She must have felt dreadfully to blame for involving your family as well. And to have known herself so taken in."

"Not to mention losing everything." Felix shook his head. "At least our family recovered, after a fashion."

"Poor Anne," Callie repeated. She studied the ring, her finger idly tracing the outline of the large, oval stone.

"I wonder why she showed herself to you so quickly?" Lady Agatha mused.

Callie looked up. "Because I'm a member of the Rycroft family, of course. Perhaps she fears Tony will be taken in by me the way she was taken in by my ancestor."

And under the circumstances, she reflected ruefully, was there not an element of truth to that? Her betrothal to Tony was as false in her mind as ever Henry's had been to Anne.

Tony raised quizzical eyebrows, his amusement stirring as his gaze lingered on Callie. He really had missed her entertaining company. "You? Take me in?" he demanded. "My dear girl, do not be absurd."

"Absurd, am I?" Callie rallied, the challenging light sparking in her eyes.

"It is not only you Anne haunts," he reminded her. "She's been with us a great many years. And as for her coming to you, I'll wager it's because of the ring."

"The ring," she repeated, and looked down at it, an unreadable expression on her face.

Did it frighten her, he wondered? She had never been one either to show her fears or to complain. She had too much pride and spirit for her own good, at times. If the ring disturbed her, she would simply make the best of it rather than return the gift he had chosen. Which decided the matter for him. He held out his hand. "I'll find you something else."

She looked up, her gaze unfocused as if her thoughts remained elsewhere. "The ring? Now who is being absurd? This will do very well."

His eyebrows rose. "You don't mind its possible association with a ghost?"

"Not with Anne." Her gaze cleared, and she looked fully at him with eyes that kindled with the glow of determination. "I'm sorry if you would rather take it back, Tony, but I would very much like to keep it."

"Keep a haunted ring?" Felix stared at her, his expression horrified. "Lord, I'd forgotten. Nerves of steel, that's what you've got, m'girl. Damme, Tony, I never thought you'd show so much sense in your choice of a bride. What, is that a blush, Callie?" He chortled in delight.

The color in her cheeks deepened. "It is only from hearing you talk such nonsense."

More likely it was from anger, Tony reflected ruefully. His prospective bride had not yet come to terms with her new role. Hardly flattering to him. All the more so, because as far as he knew, she had never been one to indulge in romantic yearnings. Did she, in fact, long for some dashing hero who could match her wit for wit, action for action? If so, she must be all too aware that the circumstances of her poverty had forced her to accept a very poor second.

Lady Agatha studied Callie with an inscrutable expression. "Would you wish to have one of the maids sleep on a trundle bed in your room?"

Callie shook her head emphatically. "Anne doesn't mean me any harm. I should like to learn more about her, though."

"You are welcome to explore our muniments room," Tony suggested, with all the air of one offering a rare treat.

"Good God," said Felix in failing accents. "What a delightful time she would have. There cannot be more than three or four hundred volumes of records and family histories in there, gathering dust and mildew," he added in an aside to Callie.

She considered this a moment, then nodded. "The very place to begin, I should think."

"So I should think not!" declared Felix. "You take my advice and give it the go-by. Devilish dull work."

"Possibly, but I shan't mind. At least the record books won't whine and fuss like certain former pupils of mine." She rose. "May I go there at once, Tony?"

Tony frowned. "Felix is quite right—as hard as that might be to believe. You—"

"Thank you," that young gentleman interrupted, offering a sweeping bow.

"—would not find it the least bit amusing," Tony went on, ignoring the interruption.

Callie waved that aside. "As long as I find it informative, I shall be well suited. May I?"

"Stubborn." He shook his head in mock despair. "You will do as you please, of course, but don't blame me if you fall asleep over the estate books."

Actually, her plan suited him very well. His agent, not to mention a large number of papers, awaited him in the estate office. He had accounts to check, and plans to approve—or disapprove—before the necessary repairs could begin. He had any number of reports and recommendations on modern agricultural methods to review. Most pressing of all, he had still to discover the exact extent of his brother's debts, both to tradesmen and to his gaming cronies. As long as Callie remained in the muniments room, he need not worry about entertaining her—or of Felix's entertaining her in some unsuitable manner in his stead.

Excusing himself, he escorted Callie on their slow way along the corridors until they reached a small apartment near the back of the great house. Here, for generations upon generations, conscientious souls had deposited every scrap of information pertaining to the history of the family or the running of the estate. Shelves lined the walls, containing record books of all sizes and descriptions. Several huge carved chests stood spaced at even intervals, bearing other articles of interest to the family history.

Callie eyed this wealth of material, her expression daunted.

Tony grinned. "What, turning craven? I hadn't thought it of you."

She directed a scornful glance at him. "Don't be idiotish." She squared her slight shoulders and waded in to do battle with the weighty tomes. As she reached the nearest shelf, she turned to regard him over her shoulder. "I don't hear you offering to help."

"Not for worlds would I deny you the pleasure of examining each and every one of those volumes for yourself. If you should discover anything of interest, I shall be in the estate room."

"And not expecting to see me, I'll wager." With that, she turned to her task.

Still smiling, Tony started to close the door, then had to open it again to let in Archimedes, the rotund black and white ruler of the lower floors. The cat strolled to the other side of the room, stretched luxuriantly, then sprawled across the sunlit patch on the carpet. At least she'd have company, Tony reflected, and headed toward the next corridor where the estate office lay.

He did not look forward to what he would undoubtedly hear from his estate manager, and with every dragging step, his heart grew heavier. Not even the presence of Harold, the aged liver and white King Charles spaniel who sprawled in the doorway, eased his lowering mood. Without moving more muscles than necessary, the dog welcomed him with thumping tail, then yawned, and resumed his nap. Tony stepped over the animal with care and made his way around the desk to where Marmaduke dozed in his chair.

The wiry little figure of Bradshaw already sat beside the desk, hard at work compiling the list of tasks to which he had attended. Unlike the dog, the agent sprang to his feet at once, but Tony waved him back to his seat, ousted the cat, and took over the chair. "How did your inspection go this morning?" he asked at once.

"Better than I had expected, my lord." Bradshaw drew off his wire-rimmed spectacles and polished them with thoughtful intensity. Not until he had restored them to the bridge of his nose did he continue. "The repairs are well under way for the worst of the cottages, but the others will need tending before winter."

"I know." It took a measure of control not to allow his frustration to color his voice. "What are the prospects for the harvest?"

"It should do well, but we've not been at our improvements long enough to make a difference. I believe your lordship's best hope lies in preventing further waste for the time being." The estate agent hesitated, then handed over a second list that lay at his side. "These are the most pressing matters."

Tony took it, his frown deepening as he settled in for a lengthy study of the reckoning of his brother's mismanagement.

He had barely begun when the door burst open and Marianne, his widowed sister-in-law, swept in, wearing an excessively becoming morning gown and clutching her reticule. She halted just over the threshold, her lovely face flushed, her expression distraught. "Here you are, Tony. I have been searching for you everywhere!"

"Have you? My apologies." He laid down the papers. "I had thought you settled in London with your mama for a fortnight, still."

"That is of no moment!" she declared.

His eyebrows rose. "Something certainly has set you in a pucker. What may I do for you?"

"Tell me it isn't true!" she cried in failing accents that would have done credit to an actress in a Cheltenham tragedy. "Tell me you have not become engaged to some penniless Nobody!"

Bradshaw, his expression harried, rose abruptly. "If you will excuse me, my lord, I have matters requiring my attention." He eased his way around the sleeping spaniel.

Tony cast him a look redolent of understanding, watched with envious eyes as his estate agent beat a strategic retreat, then turned back to his sister-in-law. With deliberation, he raised his quizzing glass and studied her tall, graceful figure, swathed in white muslin trimmed with lavender ribands. "New gown, Marianne?"

The color in her cheeks deepened to a very becoming rose. "Well, I do not see why I should not. After all, it has been almost six months since poor Lambeth died. It is time I put off my weeds. And this is still half-mourning, after all."

"Now why," he murmured, "do I hear your mama's voice?"

"You are teasing me, and indeed, it is not

kind. Not when your mama has been regaling me with this most appalling news." She stepped around the softly snoring Harold and took the chair opposite Tony. Clenching her hands, she leaned forward across the desk, her face a picture of earnestness. "Please, tell me it is not true."

"With all the will in the world, if I could. But my mama is quite right. I am engaged."

Tears started in Marianne's limpid green eyes. "How could you? Oh, Tony, and my mama—I mean *I*—have just found the most perfect heiress for you! Truly, she is just the thing, and would solve all our difficulties. No, listen," she rushed on as he started to protest, "she is the daughter of an East India nabob. Only imagine, her father is thrilled at the idea of her marrying a title, and will come down handsomely on the marriage settlements. And you shall like her, I feel certain you shall, for she is not really such an antidote."

His jaw set. "I believe I told you I am not interested in selling my name."

"But we need the money!" she cried, her voice rising in her distress.

"We wouldn't," he said gently, "if we all refrained from extravagant purchases for a little while."

Her eyes brimmed with ready tears. "You mean me. But truly, it was the most necessary of expenses." She looked down at the figured white muslin, with its tiny puff sleeves and double flounce, and ran her fingers lovingly over the skirt. "I made certain you would not begrudge it to me"

"Is that what your mama told you?"

Her chin rose in defiance. "I told you, it is time I emerged into half-mourning. Oh, Tony, you can have no idea how lowering it is to the spirits to be forever garbed in black or purple."

"I see." A vague throbbing began in his temples, and absently he rubbed the side of his head with one hand. "How much have you spent?"

A puzzled crease formed in her brow. "I have no idea. Lambeth never worried about such things, and my mama said there would be not the least need to keep track. All that matters is that I'm properly gowned."

He spoke carefully, keeping the tension from his voice. "How many have you ordered?"

"Only six. Truly it was no more than that." She regarded him with much the look of a hopeful puppy.

Propping his elbows on the desktop, he tented his fingertips and regarded her over their tops. "You must know we are already grossly encumbered. To you, the expense of the gowns may seem trifling—"

"Indeed, it does not! They are quite shocking. If Madame Celestine were not the most fashionable modiste in London, Mama vows she would take our custom elsewhere."

Tony bit back an acid rejoinder. After a moment, he managed to say with commendable calm: "I would greatly appreciate it if you would refrain from purchasing anything else until the start of next Season."

That brought a smile of relief to her bow-shaped mouth. "Oh, no, there should be no need. I told Mama I could never wear more than the six, not even for the Little Season, for you must know she plans for us to stay in Cavendish Square, if you will but allow us to open the town house. And you are not to worry about the propriety of it, for we mean to be most quiet and hardly entertain at all. If I am to meet—" She broke off with a soft exclamation, her expression stricken.

Tony's eyes narrowed. "Do you mean your mama is actually planning on launching you back into the Marriage Mart?" he demanded.

Marianne's gaze dropped to study the hands she clenched before her. "It is my duty to support my mama," she said in a subdued voice, "for you must know her jointure is the merest pittance, and my brother has nary a feather to fly with. So it is of the first importance that I contract an eligible alliance."

For a long moment, Tony regarded her in silence. "I do see," he said at last.

"Truly, it will not be so very bad. She says that when I wear the rubies—"

"The what?" he interrupted.

"The rubies." Uncertainty, tinged with no little dismay, flickered across her features. "Mama says that if I must be decked out like a crow, at least I should be a sparkling crow. And indeed, they set me off to perfection—several people have been so kind as to tell me so. And since there are none among the Lambeth jewels, surely you must see I had to purchase a set."

"How much?" Even to himself, his voice sounded hollow."

She wouldn't meet his gaze. "I have no idea. Mama says it's vulgar to discuss prices. But you need not worry, she told Rundel and Bridge to send you the bill, so you should know at any time."

"I am grateful to her," he said through gritted teeth.

Her eyes misted with her ready tears. "Oh, dear, you are going to be unpleasant about it, but indeed, I wish you would not. Truly, I did not mean to upset you."

"No." A sigh escaped him "I suppose it would be the height of foolishness to expect you to stand up to your mama."

She blinked back the moisture and rewarded him with a grateful, if watery, smile. "I knew you would understand. But only consider, we should not be in such straits if you would but marry this nabob's heiress."

The door flung open, cutting short his reply. Callie strode in, the massive black and white Archimedes cradled in her arms, her face bright and her eyes sparkling. "Tony, I have seen her again! Anne!" She stepped over the recumbent Harold with care. "She was there, in the muniments room!"

"If there ever was such a female!" remarked Felix, following her to the room but stopping short of the dog. "She's delighted at seeing a ghost. I'll tell you this, Tony, I'm glad it's you and not me who's saddling himself with this—" He broke off, staring past Tony. "Lady Lambeth," he said in choked accents. The next moment, he recovered and raised his quizzing glass, the better to study her elegant figure.

"The inconsolable widow. How touching to find you still maintaining at least some pretext of mourning."

Marianne, her face unnaturally pale, stared at him as if she were beholding the ghostly Anne. Dragging her gaze from his face, she cast a beseeching look at Tony. A stifled sob escaped her, and she brushed past them and ran from the room.

Five

"Really, Felix." Tony drew an enameled snuff box from his pocket and weighed it in his hand. "I must ask you to behave yourself."

Felix shrugged a petulant shoulder. "Pay her no heed. A lachrymose creature, forever indulging in the vapors."

"Indeed?" Tony's brows rose, and he paused in the act of taking a pinch of Bordeaux. "I had no idea you were so well acquainted with her."

"Oh, we've met from time to time in town. I have never understood why—" He broke off as the measured tread of footsteps approached down the hall. "Ah, here comes our good Durstan."

The butler came to a halt, eyeing that young gentleman with a measure of disapproval. "Your luggage has arrived, Mr. Felix."

"Yes?" Felix regarded him with gentle amusement. "But I fail to see what you expect me to do about it. Does my man not have the matter well in hand?"

"Mr. Ripton," intoned Durstan in deep disapproval, "has taken it upon himself to dispense with the aid of both James and Albert, and is now at a loss as to how to convey your portmanteaux to your chamber."

Felix sighed. "Undoubtedly they offended him." He shook his head. "You must hold me excused, dear coz. And dear Callie. I must go and see if I can untangle this muddle." With a sweeping bow for Callie, he set forth on his errand, followed by the grimly satisfied butler.

"What a delightful house party you have arranged," Callie murmured. "I take it that was your sister-in-law, returned early from London?"

"You were not privileged to see her at her best." Tony hesitated a moment before adding: "Felix has never liked her, I fear."

"Then I shall look forward to making her acquaintance without his influence. But Tony," she rushed on, returning to what was, to her, a matter of far more importance, "Anne came to me in the muniments room. And she beckoned for me to follow her!"

That arrested Tony's attention. This was certainly a new turn for Anne. For that matter, showing herself so often was unprecedented. In spite of the problems that weighed so heavily on him, he found himself intrigued. "Did you?" he demanded.

"I tried. But she drifted through the door, and by the time I was able to stand—thanks to Archimedes here," she jostled the sleepy cat that stretched from her arms upward across her left shoulder, "and gotten the door open, I couldn't see any trace of her. And I must say, if she were so urgent as to beckon, the very least she could do would be to wait for me."

"Perhaps she had expended her energy," Tony suggested, amused by Callie's air of grievance.

Callie sank onto the chair lately occupied by the estate agent, and rearranged the hefty weight of the docile feline in her lap. "That might pose a problem. How can I discover what she wants if she keeps disappearing?"

"Follow faster?"

She threw him a disgusted look. "I suppose you expect me to wait in the place I last saw her until she can return to lead me a few steps further?"

With an effort, he kept his smile from sounding in his voice. "You can have your dinner brought to you on a tray. Shall I order it now?"

"You shall not." She rose as she spoke, setting the indignant Archimedes on the chair in her stead. An exaggerated sigh escaped her. "I should have known it would be pointless talking to you."

"Unkind." He shook his head in mock sorrow. "When I have been at such pains to hit upon ways to help you."

"Completely pointless," she declared with conviction. "If you will excuse me, *my lord?*"

His eyebrows rose. "I must have offended you, indeed, to sink so low. Pray, forgive me." He caught her elbow and assisted her over the dozing Harold.

She accepted his aid willingly enough, for Harold covered a sizable portion of the threshold, then moved away. "I wish Anne could simply tell me what she wants."

"Perhaps she will. After all, you have been in the house less than twelve hours, and she has already appeared to you twice—and in a very substantial form, I might add."

A sudden gurgle of laughter escaped her. "I think if I heard her voice, I should run screaming from the room!"

"Not you." He shook his head. "You are far more likely to demand so many answers and explanations from her, she would disappear again just to escape from you."

Callie made a face at him. "You're only jealous because she's not appearing to you."

He laughed at that, but to his surprise, he had to give an extra nudge to produce that response. Could he be jealous? No, the idea was utter nonsense. Never, in all his life, had he ever given more than a passing acknowledgement to the family specter. She'd always been there; he supposed he took her for granted.

In fact, it dawned on him, it was not the ghost's inclination toward Callie that made him jealous, but Callie's for the ghost. Her eyes gleamed with her excitement over Anne. No such light brightened them at the prospect of becoming his wife. When he recalled the hero worship with which she had once honored him, he found her present indifference lowering. Well, what did he expect? She was no longer a child, and he was no longer a dashing figure fit for a young girl's romantic dreams.

They approached the Great Hall to find a

motley array of trunks, portmanteaux, and valises scattered about a tiny man who was dressed in the unmistakable costume of a gentleman's gentleman. He clutched an elegant dressing case in both hands, and issued a string of orders to which neither Durstan nor the two footmen paid any heed. Felix was nowhere to be seen.

"I thought he was going to take care of this," Callie murmured. "I wouldn't have expected him to turn craven and run."

Tony stepped forward and addressed himself to the valet. "Where is Mr. Felix?"

"Here," came Felix's voice from the Gold Salon across the hall. He emerged, followed by the plump, competent figure of Mrs. Durstan. "It seems my room has only just been prepared. Ripton," he turned to his man, "you may now see to the removal of my trappings."

Mr. Ripton turned a pained look on him. "I have been endeavoring to do so this half hour past, sir. But these—these—" He broke off, words apparently failing him. "They are unfit to handle your cases."

"That can't be helped," Tony announced with a cheerful determination that defied contradiction. "James, Albert, I want these things in—the Green Room? Yes, in the Green Room. Now." With that, he headed toward the salon from which Felix had just emerged. Behind him, he could hear the scrambling sounds of the footmen grasping pieces of luggage and Ripton's strangled protests.

"Neatly done," Callie commented, keeping pace with him.

Felix greeted him with a shaking of his head. "It saddens me to acknowledge I have never had your turn for command."

"Nor my distaste for the disorderly, it seems. You appear to have prepared for an extended stay," he nodded toward the rapidly diminishing pile of luggage.

"My intentions remain unfixed." Felix waved a vague hand. "I have vacated my lodgings—a trifling dispute with the landlord, but one I had no wish to repeat. I am, shall we say, bearing all my earthly possessions."

Which meant he had been unable to pay, Tony hazarded. Keeping his expression impassive, he said: "You may certainly store whatever you wish here, until you find more congenial rooms. And do not feel you must be in any hurry about it."

A flicker of something that might have been relief passed over Felix's countenance. "I felt certain you would not mind. But I have no intention of remaining here myself many days. Now, I think I had best see to the ordering of my chamber. Not that I don't trust Ripton implicitly, mind, but it would be unconscionable to be late for dinner. I should never so offend your dear mama's cook." With that, he headed for the stairs, where Ripton picked his fastidious way, still clutching the dressing case.

"Another crisis averted," said Callie. "But I suppose he is right, and we ought to dress for dinner. Is this cook truly such a paragon?"

"I have only once encountered his superior," Tony assured her. "And my mama has been trying to obtain his services ever since."

Callie shook her head. "She'd best take care, or risk losing her own treasure." She, too, started for the stairs.

Tony hurried to catch up to her, cursing silently at the pain caused by this effort. Callie at once slowed, which, although making it easier for him, did little to raise his opinion of himself, which only irked him even more. Part of the reason he had selected Callie as his bride was her ability to manage on her own and not need him dancing attendance on her. So why did it vex him so much that he could not keep pace with her?

Grimly, he escorted her to her chamber. Whether he did this to prove to himself—and Callie—that he could walk that far, or out of some unformed hope that he might glimpse the ghostly flickering of Anne, he couldn't be certain. Either way, he found little satisfaction. Callie merely thanked him, assured him it had been quite unnecessary for she knew perfectly well where her chamber lay, and went inside. Anne didn't even offer him that much. Annoyed, he retraced his steps to the landing, then headed down the Gallery to his own chamber, where he found his man waiting in stoic patience to assist him in dressing.

This he accomplished quickly. After assuring himself with a rapid survey in the cheval glass that he presented a quiet but elegant appearance, he made his way downstairs. To his relief, he found no one else in the Blue Salon.

As Tony poured himself a glass of Madeira, though, Felix strode into the room, his slight figure arrayed in an elegant coat of mulberry velvet with a nipped-in waist and broad lapels. An opulent floral waistcoat brought an instant protest from Tony; Felix ignored the pithy comment with an imperviousness that could only have arisen from long custom. "Is that part of the lot your grandfather laid down?" Felix demanded as he joined him.

Tony eyed him with a sudden mischievous gleam. "See if you can tell." He handed him the glass and fixed another for himself.

Felix inhaled the bouquet, then took a tentative sip. For several seconds he swished the deep ruby liquid about in his mouth, then swallowed.

Tony leaned against the back of the sofa, watching his relative in amusement. "Well?"

Felix directed a pained look at him. "One cannot rush these things, dear coz." He sipped again. "No. I fear I shall have to have more than one glass to be certain."

"Meaning you know perfectly well it's my grandfather's." Tony nodded. "I'll tell you what. I will present you with a half dozen bottles if you can manage to remain civil to Marianne."

Felix's eyes narrowed. "For how long? Oh, very well, I will do my best. But I make no promises."

The door opened, and Felix's face brightened as Callie, looking quite fetching in the amber open-robed gown that boasted a low decolletage and a single flounce, breezed into the room. "Am I late?" she asked. "No, your mama is not yet down. That's a relief."

"Negus?" Tony reached for the decanter.

"You should be offering her champagne,"

declared Felix. He took Callie's hand and raised it to his lips. "My dear, why didn't you warn me you intended to grow into such a great beauty?"

"Why didn't you warn me you intended to grow into such an unconscionable flirt?" she responded promptly, but made no demur when he led her to the sofa and settled himself at her side.

In fact, Tony noted in displeasure, she seemed to enjoy his gallantries, which grew more extravagant by the minute. The arrival of his mother, accompanied by Marianne, provided a less than welcome diversion, for he had the privilege of seeing his sister-in-law elegantly gowned in another new, and undoubtedly costly, creation of a vastly becoming green silk.

Felix, observing her arrival through half-lidded eyes, murmured: "What, not dripping roses this evening? You disappoint me, Cousin Marianne."

The widow flushed and turned away, accepting with patent gratitude the glass held out to her by Tony.

"She wisely leaves the floral tributes to your waistcoat," Callie declared coolly, and rose as Lady Agatha presented her formally to Marianne. Callie instantly complimented her on the gown, which threw Marianne into further dismay.

Fortunately, Durstan arrived to announce dinner, and Tony was able to usher the party across the hall into the small dining room. His mother had settled the difficult table arrangement by placing Callie at Tony's right and Felix next to her. Marianne occupied the opposite side of the table across from Callie, as far from Felix's stinging tongue as could be managed.

Felix, for the most part, ignored Marianne. But that brought Tony little satisfaction. Instead, his rackety relative concentrated on showering the most extravagant compliments on Callie. Tony might have been amused by Felix's absurdities, had not Callie, to his utter amazement, responded by flirting right back.

He didn't mind in the least, he assured himself. In fact, he'd find the whole charade amusing if it were not for the fact that in his role as her protector, he could not place complete reliance on Felix to know where to draw the line—or worse, on Felix's not being serious. By no stretch of the imagination could he consider Felix to be a suitable husband for Callie. He glowered at his plate and stabbed a perfectly innocent collop of veal. He hadn't counted on flirtations as one of the vexatious problems attached to taking care of her.

His mother, he noted in further irritation, made no attempt to curb Felix's flowery tongue. Perhaps she encouraged anything that shielded Marianne from insult, thus preventing an uncomfortable scene. Or she might be more devious than that. His mama had been against his offering for the girl. Did she hope Felix might captivate Callie instead, thus ending what she considered a mistaken betrothal? If so, she'd be disappointed. Callie had more sense than to be taken in by Felix's Spanish coin.

At last the meal drew to a close, and Lady Agatha rose, catching the glances of the other two ladies. "Shall we remove to the Blue Salon?" She exited the room, followed by Callie and Marianne.

Felix breathed a sigh of relief. "Not one barbed word did I utter to her," he declared with intense pride.

"Not one word did you utter to her at all," Tony shot back.

Felix awarded him a sly smile. "Yes, I thought you'd be pleased."

Tony bit back the retort that he was not in the least pleased. Instead, as Durstan placed the decanters of brandy and port on the table, he asked: "Do you care to play billiards this evening?"

Felix raised his eyebrows. "What? Anxious to keep me away from Marianne? Have no fear. For your sake, dear coz, I will try to keep my tongue in check." He took an appreciative sip of the smooth ruby liquid in his glass. "And as much as I should like to linger here, I feel it is our duty to join the ladies."

This they did after only two more glasses, leaving Tony wondering how to keep Felix and Marianne apart when he also felt it his duty to curb the growing intimacy between Felix and Callie.

As they neared the Salon, the melodic strains of the pianoforte reached them. Marianne, Tony assumed, and was surprised to discover it was in fact Callie who sat at the keyboard with Archimedes curled in her lap and Marmaduke draped over the top of the instrument, one paw hanging down toward the keys, his avid gaze fixed on her moving fingers. Another of the cats, the gray Percival, curled against the recumbent form of Harold, who dozed in blissful canine contentment before the fire.

Marianne looked up from her position beside Lady Agatha on the sofa and blinked at Felix. "I was not aware that the gamesters had taken to aping the Tulips. Or did one of the dandies' less successful tailors move into the neighborhood off St. James's Street?"

Felix froze, but only for a moment. His eyes gleamed as he picked up her gauntlet. "Is that another of Celestine's creations? I always thought she was overrated."

"I see you have had card tables set up," Tony said quickly. "Marianne, will you join my mother and me in a game of loo?"

"Oh, noble of you," murmured Felix with a grin, and moved past him into the room. "Callie, your neglectful future husband has left you to me. Do you play piquet?"

"It's been an age! I shall bore you dreadfully," she declared, but rose at once from the pianoforte to join him, bringing Archimedes with her.

"That," Felix assured her as he drew out a chair, "you could never do."

The footmen had placed the tables sufficiently apart so that one group's conversation wouldn't distract the play of the other. It also, Tony noted with satisfaction, inhibited the casual tossing back and forth of veiled insults. The drawback, though, he quickly discovered, was that it made it difficult to intervene when Felix got out of hand.

The two at the other table laughed just then,

drawing his attention, and he caught Felix's eye.

"Don't let her fool you, Tony," Felix called gaily. "She's an expert player! And here she has been trying to convince me she has had no recent practice."

"Well, I haven't!" Callie pointed out.

Felix shook his head, mournfully. "It's my opinion you're a regular Captain Sharp! But you'll find I'm no pigeon for your plucking. Come, give me another hand."

Tony, feeling oddly left out, watched as they resumed play. What business of Felix's was it to sound proud of Callie's abilities? If anyone should have pride in her, it should be himself. Annoyed, he returned his attention to his mother and Marianne, only to be diverted again by a bark of surprised laughter from Felix, followed by his exclamation of "Well done!"

"What on earth are you two about?" Lady Agatha demanded.

"He has taught me to deal from the bottom of the deck!" Callie called.

"And she did it to the manner born, too," Felix declared in the tone of a mentor showing off a prize pupil.

Tony felt his hackles rise. "Do you intend to teach her to fuzz the cards, as well?"

Felix considered. "What do you say, Callie? Would you like that?"

Her eyes sparkled. "Of all things. Just think of the fun I could have. Only," she added, throwing Tony a mischievous look, "I suspect it is something I ought not to know."

Felix chuckled. "Of a certainty it is not. Nor should any of us, for that matter. But I never let a little matter like that stand in my way. Why, we—"

"Tony!" Callie interrupted him. She stared across the room, her expression intent. Archimedes, in her lap, sat up rigid, whiskers a-twitch.

Suddenly alert, Tony followed the direction of her gaze to where a ghostly flame flickered near the far wall. As he watched, it moved toward them, hesitated, then retreated. For the briefest moment it shimmered, and he thought he could make out the hazy outline of a figure.

A small, wavering scream escaped Marianne. The girl rose on trembling legs, and Felix sprang to her side, grasping her about the shoulders as she wavered. A chill seeped through the room.

As abruptly as it had appeared, the apparition vanished.

Marianne gave a small sob, and Felix drew her closer for a moment, then pressed her gently into her chair. "What? Afraid of a ghost?" he rallied. "She's lived here a great deal longer than you have, and has yet to do anyone any harm."

"She wants something!" Callie hugged the indignant cat to her in patent frustration. "And I am going to find out what it is!"

"You cannot!" cried Marianne in failing accents.

"What? Your sensibilities too fine?" Felix asked, resuming hostilities. "Helping a ghost sounds to me like a delightful pastime for a

house party. My dear Cousin Agatha, you have
my compliments on a most unusual entertainment."

"Are you sure that's wise?" Tony asked Callie.
Not that he wouldn't like to see Anne helped,
if she needed it, but why did Anne make Callie—not a member of her own family but a relative of the man who had betrayed her—the
object of her attentions? Yet he sensed no danger from the ghostly visitation. Only longing.

Still, this was not something Callie should do
on her own. Which meant, he suspected, he
would be put to considerable effort on the
ghost's behalf. It would be better if this had
happened in a few months' time, or even next
year, when he had dealt with the worst of the
estate's current problems. The last thing he
needed right now was the past demanding his
attention as well.

"It need not disturb you," Callie said, as if
she'd read his mind. "I know you have no time
to spare, and Felix will be only too delighted
to help."

"Will he?" Marianne's voice still quavered,
but she made a game attempt not to miss this
opportunity to slight her tormentor. "I thought
Cousin Felix aided no one but himself."

Tony's gaze rested on Callie. What if she were
right, and Anne did want—or need—something from them? The possibility intrigued him.

Even more, he realized, he was intrigued by
the soft flush that suffused Callie's cheeks. She
was quite lovely; that fact came to him as a startling revelation. Her determination to help the
ghost lent a luster to her speaking eyes, and a

glow that warmed her normally acerbic manner. He found himself fascinated.

Callie, it dawned on him, was no longer simply the capable and forthright little girl he had known. She had grown into a young woman, and must now have a young woman's desires and dreams. He had done her a grave injustice to assume she would be content with a wreck like him, just because they were friends. She deserved so very much more. It would be best for her if he could find some monies to settle on her, so she could feel free to draw back from their engagement.

The thought left an oddly cold, empty sensation in the pit of his stomach.

Six

Pale early morning light filtered through a crack in the drapes, spilling across the bed from around which Callie had drawn back the muslin curtains. Even before she opened her eyes, the certainty dawned on her that she was not alone in the room. Anne hovered somewhere near. She sat up, her gaze darting about, but she caught only a final flicker of the ghostly flame as it vanished. Anne didn't beckon, this time. Had she just popped in to say good morning?

Sinking back among the pillows, Callie enjoyed the unfamiliar luxury of not dreading the program of routine dullness that normally awaited her upon awakening. She snuggled beneath the downy softness of the comforter and allowed her thoughts to drift over the events of the previous day: seeing Tony again, being whisked from her hated position to the elegancies of the Grange, Tony's insulting proposal, the lingering presence of the ghostly Anne. So much had happened, and all in the span of only a few short hours.

Then there was Felix, a devil-may-care youth

who had grown into a charming ne'er-do-well. Thoughts of Felix led her naturally to Marianne, a timid and unhappy girl. What caused the animosity between the pair? Felix, he of the flowery tongue and insouciant flummery, wasted no opportunity to drive a barb into this unequal opponent. No casual dislike drew forth such an attack. And Marianne responded with tears—unless she had time to prepare, in which case she managed to meet insult with insult.

To Callie, that sounded like love.

She considered the matter, and found it plausible. Marianne, the penniless widow. Felix, the wastrel gamester. Financially, they were not in the least suited. Their best defense might be to keep the other at the greatest distance possible. A sound solution, if not a happy one.

But why couldn't sound solutions be happy ones as well?

Restless, she tossed back the covers and rose. The maid Jenny apparently had no idea her charge would wake so early. That suited Callie. She didn't crave a cup of hot cocoa and a roll before she could contemplate her day. She selected the newly pressed muslin round dress from the cupboard, dressed herself with the ease of long practice, and headed down the stairs to see if she could find the breakfast parlor.

The younger of the two footmen—Albert, she remembered—gave her escort. As they crossed the Great Hall, Marmaduke sauntered out of the Gold Salon. He spotted them, dropped to a crouch, and began to stalk the flounced hem of Callie's gown. Callie, watching with amusement, gave the fabric a twitch, sending the cat skittering sideways. It recovered, then settled, facing the opposite direction, thus proving it had no interest in her whatsoever. Still, as they approached the sunny chamber on the south side of the house, she was aware of the velvet-soft footsteps following in her wake.

She thanked Albert, then entered the apartment, being careful not to shut the inquisitive Marmaduke's tail in the door. Tony, who already sat at the table, looked up from his mug of ale. His brooding frown eased at sight of her, leaving his features merely strained.

"Good morning," she said brightly. She waited for the cat to cross in front of her, then headed to the sideboard where an impressive array of covered chafing dishes awaited her inspection.

Tony fended off Marmaduke's attempt to clamber ungracefully into his lap. "I don't remember inviting you to join us," he informed the feline. "And you," he added to Callie, "are certainly up early."

"Long habit." She lifted a lid at random, and the heavenly aroma of eggs coddled in an herbed cream sauce rose to greet her. "With you, too, I should imagine. Oliver always said the worst part of army life was that he was expected to be out of bed at some ridiculously early hour."

Marmaduke accepted his defeat and scrambled into another chair. Tony turned back to his ale. "I have much to do," he said shortly.

He had, she knew. She selected a slice of ham at random, while her thoughts focused on her old friend. All that worry wasn't good for him. He'd grown too sober, too full of troubles. He needed diversion. She turned to regard him through lowered lids. "I have a great deal to do, as well. I meant what I said, you know. I want to help Anne. She was in my room again this morning," she added, dropping what she felt certain would be bait.

Instead of interest kindling in his tired eyes, Tony's brow snapped down. "That cannot make you comfortable. If you will not allow one of the maids to sleep in there, at least let us move you to another chamber."

"Do not be absurd!" she snapped, her ready irritation flaring. "What a poor creature you must think me, to be afraid of a little thing like a ghost. I assure you, I am no such thing."

His lips twitched. "I beg your pardon."

She sniffed. "And so you should." Her temper faded as quickly as it had soared. "The more I think about it, the more I am convinced that Anne wants something—and from me, specifically, not just anyone."

"What?" He eyed her with suspicion.

"I don't know." Callie frowned. "Henry Rycroft treated her shamefully. Since he was my relative, perhaps she wants me to make amends in some way for his betrayal."

Tony's head jerked up, and his hand clenched the handle of his ale mug. "Callie, you wretch, if you're saying that to tip me a rise, I swear—"

"Tony!" Her eyes opened wide in mock horror. "What would your poor mama say if she heard you using boxing cant in my presence?"

"She'd probably rip up at me for expressing myself too mildly," came his prompt response. "Now, if you would be serious for a moment—"

"But I am. Look, Tony. She has definitely singled me out. She wants me to do something for her, and I intend to find out what. And to do it."

"What if it's dangerous?"

Her eyes kindled. "Do you think I'd run shy? My family honor may very well be at stake here. If you have no desire to help me, that's your affair. I don't need you. I can manage very well on my own, thank you."

"You can't manage anything on your own! When I think of the scrapes you got yourself into—"

"Me? When you know perfectly well it was I, who was six years your junior, who thought of the nackiest ways to extricate us all from the bumblebroths you led us into!"

"*I* led? Who thought of the worst of them, pray tell?"

"Worst? You had nothing but praise for me, at the time."

"Well, I don't now." He glowered at her. "I'll thank you to remember that you currently are staying under my roof, not to mention the fact you are betrothed to me—"

"Currently," she snapped back.

"—which makes you my responsibility," he finished, glaring all the harder at her. "And I also," he added as one aggrieved, "promised Oliver I would look after you, God help me. I will not have you engaging in any freakish starts without my company! Is that understood?"

"You don't want to miss the fun?" she asked sweetly.

"You're as incorrigible as a resty colt!"

Her chin thrust out. "Considering what a wonderful opinion you have of my character, I'm amazed you offered for me!"

His eyes flashed. "And I'm amazed we quit arguing long enough for you to accept. Lord, when I think I only wanted to live a quiet life!"

A gasping laugh escaped her. She saw his anger flare, but she couldn't help herself. "You? A quiet life? Absolutely not! Some part of you knew better. You'd be bored to distraction within a se'nnight if you tried anything so idiotish." She tilted her head to one side, considering him. "Do you think that is really why you offered for me? To assure yourself of a very *un*quiet life?"

"At the moment, I would settle for a very quiet breakfast."

"Too late, you've already finished yours. You may now escape me by attending to the estate matters that I feel certain are awaiting your attention. And I," she added loftily, "while you are pursuing your quiet life, shall engage upon an adventure."

"What the devil have you in mind?" he demanded.

"Helping Anne, of course. I shall seek the attics and search for anything that might tell me more about her."

"You call that an adventure?" Abruptly, he grinned. "I wish you joy of the dust." He tossed off the last of his ale and left her to her morning's entertainment.

Callie watched in satisfaction as the door swung closed behind him. That flare of temper would do him a world of good. It hadn't done her any harm, either. As she turned once more to the selection of her breakfast, she wondered how long he would be able to concentrate on estate matters before his longing to join her search got the better of him, and he joined her among the trunks and boxes of long forgotten relics.

Tony strode down the corridor, emotions in a turmoil. How could any chit as tiny as that one so completely disrupt his life, cut up his peace, and throw him into a raging passion one minute, only to reduce him to helpless laughter the next? Because she was Callie, of course. Volatile, unpredictable, a raging termagant: with grim satisfaction, he ticked off a catalogue of her faults. She could make him dearly long to strangle her, then disarm him utterly with a rueful apology.

He slowed. He'd been right about one thing, at least: she didn't need him at all. She could amuse herself, find some mystery or occupation on which to expend her boundless energy. He need never worry about her feeling dull-witted and bored. So why didn't that fact fill him with satisfaction?

He entered the estate room, found it temporarily unoccupied by the industrious Bradshaw, and settled behind the desk with the massive lists of repairs before him. These he attacked with worthy determination, but restlessness got the better of him within a very few minutes. He didn't want to be sitting and reading reports, he wanted to be out in his fields, among his tenants, seeing for himself what needed to be done. The knowledge that any action he could take would do little to improve the condition of the farms only frustrated him further. He tugged the bellpull, and when the breathless James hurried to answer the summons, he sent the footman to order his curricle brought round as soon as his pair could be harnessed. Seeing the estate might only depress him further, but it was far better than simply reading lists.

The fresh air lifted his mood only until he neared the home farm. From that point on, his worries took over. When, some two hours later, he returned to the house and handed his pair over to his groom, his spirits rode at low ebb from all he had seen and heard. Yet grimly he clung to the hopes of the harvest that would begin the following day. He could do little now, but wait, and trust the dark clouds that gathered on the horizon would keep their distance.

He headed with tired, dragging steps up the stairs toward his chambers to change from the clothes to which horse hairs still clung. As he turned down the Gallery, Marianne emerged from her room, gowned in a new riding habit of sapphire blue. She presented an admirable picture in it, he reflected, and it probably came with a price to match.

She saw him and halted, her expression stricken. "Tony," she said in a small voice.

He nodded to her, determined to allow no reproaches to escape his lips.

"I—I thought I would go riding," she said. "I intended to ask Miss Rycroft to accompany me, but I could find her nowhere."

"I believe she planned to spend the day in the attics."

"In the—" A nervous giggle escaped her. "Oh, no, Tony, that's doing it too brown. I won't swallow such a plumper as that. If you should see her, I should like it of all things if she would join me." With that, she hurried past and ran lightly down the stairs.

He watched her progress with a thoughtful frown. It was highly improper of her to be in colors, but he couldn't blame her desire to be free of her mourning. Yet at the moment, she bore little appearance of being happy, or even content, in her widowed state. She dreaded her mama's plans to tie her into a profitable marriage, of course.

He continued along the hall toward his room, frowning. If the estate were not grossly encumbered, she would have no need of another marriage—or at least a better excuse to put her mama off. His own marriage to this nabob's heiress would do the trick. It would free him, as well, from worries about his beloved Grange. Even Callie would be free to look where she chose for a husband, for he could settle a dowry on her.

And why, he wondered, did this last thought cause him sudden pain? He considered the matter, and found that he enjoyed the vitality Callie brought to the house.

Suddenly, he wanted to know where she was, how she'd spent her morning. It seemed inconceivable that she still might be in the attics, for he could imagine no more boring or uncomfortable a task than the one she'd contemplated. Yet this was Callie, he reminded himself. He'd never yet known her to run shy. She very well might remain at her work, either until she unraveled the mystery of Anne's beckoning, or until someone dragged her away. A pang of guilt assailed him at the realization that while he'd been driving about the farms in the fresh air, she'd been closed away in the attics, all alone.

Or had she been alone? He hadn't seen Felix about.

Somehow, that decided the matter. He had done all he could that morning for the estate. Spending more hours in the office would accomplish little. Now it was his duty to prevent Callie from exhausting herself, or worse, making herself ill from the dust.

He altered his course and proceeded to the back stairs that led to the attics. The climb proved every bit as difficult as he'd feared, and long before he reached the top his leg pained him. For several minutes, he rested on the landing before making his way along the dark, narrow hallway to the only door that stood ajar.

Little light filtered into the long, low room that he entered; motes of dust swirled in the few rays that penetrated the grime-encrusted windows. On the far side, separated from the doorway by piles of forgotten treasures and broken furniture, Callie sat on a chair that kilted at a sharp angle. She had changed into her serviceable brown merino, and from what he could see of the state of the attic, it had been a good idea. A tray with the remnants of a light nuncheon sat on a flat-topped trunk at her side, and a box of papers perched precariously on her knees. Another trunk, its lid thrown back, stood before her. Tony advanced a cautious step into the room, and sneezed from the onslaught of dust.

Callie's head jerked up, and she frowned. "What on earth are you doing here?" she demanded.

"Sneezing. Lord, how can you stand to be in here?"

She ignored that. "You shouldn't have climbed up here. Really, at times I wonder if you have any sense at all, Tony. All those stairs! If you aren't going to allow your knee to rest, how do you expect it to heal?" She set the papers aside and rose to thread her way through the mounded clutter to join him. The passage of her skirts stirred up more dust, setting them both sneezing.

"Haven't you more sense than to stay in this?" he demanded when he could speak again.

"It wouldn't be a problem if you'd have the lumber rooms cleaned once in a while," came her prompt response.

"Why on earth should we? We're already understaffed, and very few of our guests choose to spend their time up here."

"One cannot blame them."

He regarded her in half exasperation, half

amusement. "You might do well to follow their example."

"I could hardly have the entire contents of the attics carried downstairs, could I? I've been trying to sort through all of this to find just what I need."

"I don't see why you need any of it."

The light of battle kindled in her eyes. "No, you wouldn't, would you? Maybe that's why Anne had to come to me for help."

"I don't see where you're helping anyone, just sitting up here sneezing."

"I've made a great deal of progress!"

"In what? Practicing your sneezing?"

She cast him a withering look. "In finding things from Anne's time. That entire trunk over there, for example. And that one, as well. Which you might notice if you stopped ripping up at me for a moment."

"If you've found something, what are you doing still up here?"

For a moment, her mouth worked in indignation; then she burst out laughing. "You are absolutely impossible. I have no desire to stay up here a moment longer than necessary—and I certainly don't see where it's getting me anywhere standing here arguing with you. Since your ancestors lacked the foresight to install bellpulls up here, you would be of the greatest help if you went back downstairs and summoned the footmen to carry these for me." She gestured toward the trunks.

"Will you also come down?"

"In a little. I want to check a few more boxes."

"They can wait. You've set aside more than enough to keep you busy for days. Come down now."

"And how will the footmen know which boxes I want? No, the sooner you send them to me, the sooner I can get out of this dust-ridden room."

Tony considered arguing, but his knowledge of Callie warned him this was an occupation they could continue, fruitlessly, for the remainder of the day. Resigned, he accepted the box of bundled letters she thrust into his hands, and made his way once more down the stairs. After dispatching the footmen to Callie's aid, he resisted the impulse to follow them. Instead, he made his way to the Blue Salon, where he'd requested the motley collection of boxes and trunks be brought, and sat down to wait.

Callie appeared in a surprisingly short time bearing another box, her gown liberally covered in dust and spiderwebs, her long hair wisping free from her no-longer neat chignon.

He greeted her with an urbane smile. "Much better, don't you think?"

She regarded the room with a critical eye. "There should be sufficient light," she agreed.

"And you are guaranteed not to be suffocated by the dust."

First Albert, then James followed her into the room, each bearing a small trunk. These they deposited next to the boxes on one side of the hearth, then departed to gather their next load.

Callie regarded the growing pile with dubious pleasure. "One would think we might learn something from all this," she said, but with an ill-concealed note of skepticism.

"It would be a marvelous thing if we did not," he agreed. "If only the gossip of the day. Or how many spiders have taken up their residence in the trunks."

"And won't your mama be delighted to find we have invaded her salon."

"For convenience," he said smoothly. "I made certain you would enjoy being at your task after dinner. But now," he added before she could produce a cutting retort, "you will take a break and walk for a little in the fresh air. Or would you prefer to ride? Marianne went out a little while ago. You might easily catch her up."

Callie, a gleam in her eyes, tilted her head to one side and eyed him speculatively. "What I'd really like is to drive your grays. I haven't had the opportunity of handling the ribbons in ages."

He hesitated only a moment. He'd taken them out himself only a little while ago, but they had certainly not grown tired, only had the frisky edge taken from them. It should be safe. "Very well," he said.

Callie eyed him with suspicion. "You're not going to argue about it?"

His amusement stirred. "I? Argue? With you? I've never heard such a plumper."

"And you will let me handle the ribbons?"

"Unless you've turned into a regular slow-top."

"Beast. As if I would." Without further comment—or perhaps to prevent his making any—she hurried from the room.

He had barely sent a message to the stable when she hurried down the stairs to join him, dressed in a riding habit of a very becoming emerald green. Within a few minutes, his groom Grimsby drove the grays to the door, and Tony escorted her outside and assisted her onto the seat. She seemed oblivious to his own trouble of climbing in as she settled her skirts about her, then relieved the dubious Grimsby of control of the horses. As soon as Tony seated himself at her side and dismissed the groom, she gave the pair the office and set forth at a spanking pace.

"You're out of practice," he protested, calling her to book. "And my grays are mettlesome at the best of times." The gleam in her eyes warned him, and he caught his balance as they exited the gate at far too fast a clip.

"Not a scratch," she informed him with pride. "I haven't lost my old precision of eye."

"Precision of what?" he demanded. "I taught you to drive, I'll thank you to remember. Yes, and now I come to think of it, the last time you pulled that stunt, you left a long scratch along the side, and nearly ditched us into the bargain."

"I did no such thing! And if we are to talk of cow-handedness, do you recall the time you tried to hunt the squirrel and wound up overturning your gig?"

He fixed her with an admonitory eye. "That was Oliver. I was merely a passenger."

"So you tried to make me believe. But I had

the story from old Mrs. Ornasham herself, for it was her carriage you'd tried to graze, and she said she hadn't laughed so much in an age."

A rueful smile tugged at the corners of his mouth. "Lord, I'd almost forgotten that," he said, and launched into another reminiscence.

They continued arguing amicably over old times for some while, until they at last turned and started back toward the house. As they swept around a bend in the road, they spotted two riders beneath the oaks on the verge. Marianne and Felix looked up, and Felix raised a hand in acknowledgement.

Marianne turned her mount and headed toward the curricle. Even at that distance, Tony could see her face, pale and angry; she looked perilously near to tears. Tony cast a furious glare at Felix, but his cousin merely shrugged an uninterested shoulder, gave them a farewell wave, and headed his horse across the field at an easy canter.

"What a little beauty," Callie declared in admiration of Marianne's mount, neatly providing a distraction. "How are her paces?"

Marianne blinked back moisture from her eyes. "Well enough," she managed, but her voice sounded choked.

Callie nodded. "Then you must have chosen her. Reginald always liked the flashiest mounts, though they'd invariably be found to be touched in the wind or too short in the pastern, and would give you the most jolting ride. Do you head back to the house? Then do not let us detain you. We have a stop to make."

"We do?" Tony asked as Marianne spurred her horse forward.

"Certainly. Right here. She needs a moment to recover."

"Thoughtful of you," Tony said.

"You mean how vexatious of Felix." An odd note sounded in her voice.

He shot her a quick glance, but could read nothing in her expression. Still, it left him with the distinct impression she understood more of this unfortunate situation than he did, and that irritated him.

Callie's plans for helping Anne dominated the conversation at dinner. This necessitated the removal of the gentlemen along with the ladies immediately following the meal, with Felix bearing the decanter of brandy with him. Announcing himself satisfied to watch, that gentleman settled at one of the card tables with Lady Agatha for a game of piquet. Marianne, thus neatly excluded, joined Tony and Callie beside the collection of boxes and trunks. Tony seated himself in a chair near the fire with the spaniel Harold lying at his feet. Callie and Marianne sat across from him on the sofa, each taking a box of letters to check the dates. Marmaduke, Archimedes, and even the gray Percival perched on various choice locations where they could keep the activity under sleepy observation.

A little over an hour and a half passed in fruitless inspection, until Tony suddenly found himself holding a bundle that appeared to have been written at the correct time by one of Anne's relatives who was making the Grand

Tour. A lively account, he noted, though the correspondent never once made any reference to events taking place at the Grange. Tony looked up to tell Callie of his discovery, only to see her sitting in unnatural stillness, staring pensively at the mirror. She hugged her light shawl tightly about her shoulders.

It had become a trifle cool, despite the blazing hearth. Even as the thought flashed through his mind, a chill seeped through him. An otherworldly chill. The cats, he realized, had risen to half crouches and stared fixedly in the same direction as Callie. Suddenly alert, he, too, turned to gaze at the mirror.

The hazy face of a young woman stared back at him, reflected in the silvered surface. Even as he watched, a wavering flame filled the image. She raised her ghostly hand and, with the slightest of movements, beckoned. A sense of loss filled him, accompanied by urgency and a plea for help so strong as to almost overwhelm him. As the vision faded, a muffled sob seemed to emerge from the mirror, rising to a wail only to dissipate into eerie silence.

Seven

Callie shivered, and with an effort dragged her gaze from the now-blank mirror. Instinctively, she turned to Tony. "Did you hear that?" Her voice came out barely above a whisper.

Tony, his gaze still fixed on the glass, nodded slowly, as one bemused.

"Hear what?" Marianne looked up from the letter she perused.

Callie stared at her, then at Lady Agatha and Felix, who sat engrossed in their game of cards, oblivious to all else. "You didn't hear a cry?" she demanded of Marianne.

"No." Bewildered, the girl looked from Callie to Tony. "Did I miss something?"

"Only a visitation by Anne," Tony assured her.

"A—" Marianne paled.

"And you really heard it?" Callie demanded of Tony. "That—that unearthly cry?"

"I did." His voice sounded distant, as if he only partially attended to her words.

Callie's gaze dropped to the box of folded papers, yellowed and stained with age, that remained on her lap. "She didn't point to these," she said.

"I noticed." He turned his thoughtful regard on Callie. "She beckoned."

Callie swallowed. "I wasn't just imagining it?"

"Not unless imagination is contagious."

"Apparently," Callie said slowly, "whatever she wants is not to be found in these boxes, or she would have pointed to them—don't you think?"

"I do." His thoughtful gaze strayed back to the mirror. "I think she wants us to go somewhere."

"But *where?*"

A sudden gleam of amusement replaced the seriousness in his eyes. "I hesitate to repeat my best suggestion, since you took it in ill part before."

"You mean follow her?"

He inclined his head. "On the whole, it seems easier than sorting through mounds of moldering papers."

"Possibly." She regarded him with misgivings. "But I've never been very good at stepping inside mirrors."

His eyebrows rose, issuing a challenge. "We can but try."

Callie accepted with alacrity. She set the box she held on the floor and sprang to her feet, toppling Percival from the edge of her skirts as she did so. For a long moment, she stood before the mirror which hung above a small pier table to the right of the hearth.

"The mirror seems most likely, since that's where we saw her," Tony said as he joined her.

Callie nodded. "But if there's a priest's hole

or some such thing, that would more likely be attached to the hearth, wouldn't it?"

He lifted the bottom of the mirror, and it moved easily away from the wall. No hinges, nothing to show it covered a secret hiding place. Frowning, he set it gently back into place.

"What are you about?" his mother demanded.

While Callie continued to explore the wall, Tony explained to the others. Lady Agatha joined them at once, followed by Felix.

"I've never heard of any sliding panel," his mother announced in tones that implied that if she hadn't heard of it, it would not be permitted to exist.

"Yet it seems likely something may be here." Tony stooped to examine the hearth. "We'll have to wait until the fire has gone out." He grasped the poker and shoved the logs aside, scattering them from the grate.

"The maid who will have to clean that won't thank you," Callie warned.

That brought a smile to his lips. "She'd like it less if she found Anne sitting in it tomorrow morning, waiting for us to help her."

A nervous giggle escaped Marianne. "Do you think she would?"

"Felix," Tony said quickly, thus forestalling any cutting remark on that gentleman's part, "will you bring that candelabrum? Yes, and if you'll hold it up here?" He bent to examine the mantel.

Callie moved to the other side, her fingers feeling along the top of the wooden structure, checking every carved knob or flower to see if anything moved. At last she stood back, frowning.

Tony looked across at her. "Nothing?"

"But she's beckoning, calling us into the—" She broke off. "Or *through* the mirror."

Felix, who had retired to a chair to watch, raised his eyebrows. "I thought you'd already covered that."

Callie shook her head. "When you go through something, you usually come out on the other side."

"The—" Tony stared at her. "The other side." He started for the door.

Callie reached it first. "It's another salon, isn't it?" She led the way along the corridor and dragged open the next door. Darkness greeted her, and with a vexed exclamation she turned back. Before she had retraced more than a dozen steps, Lady Agatha emerged from the Blue Salon, a branch of lighted candles in each hand. Callie took these with heartfelt thanks, then carried them carefully to where Tony awaited her at the entrance of the next room. He took one of the candelabra from her and set about lighting the tapers that stood ready in the darkened salon. In a few moments, a warm glow of illumination surrounded them.

Callie strode to the hearth, placed the candelabrum she carried on the mantel, then turned back to face the room. "Do you think she wants us in here? Or in another room farther along?"

"We can wait and see if she appears." Tony

joined her by the fireplace, his thoughtful gaze resting on the wall.

Leaning down, Callie examined a section of carving. "Nothing looks out of place—but then it wouldn't, or it would never have remained secret. Why can't Anne simply point to the right spot?"

He leaned across her, reaching for a boss which refused to give under pressure. His hand brushed hers as he drew back, and the contact startled her, almost as if he'd given her a shock. He stood very close, she realized. If she leaned her head just an inch or two to the right, it would press against his shoulder. He'd always had such very broad shoulders; the thought flitted through her mind. When she'd been young, and indulged in the foolishness of romantic daydreams, she'd considered him the ideal of how a young gentleman should look.

Had that changed? An unfamiliar warmth suffused her cheeks and beyond, spreading throughout her body. Confused, she moved a step away from him under the pretense of studying the side of the mantel. What odd fancies entered her mind this night. She'd long ago outgrown her girlhood infatuation for him. This ridiculous proposal of his—along with being once more in his home—had roused memories, that was all. She liked him very well, of course, but no other emotions stirred in her breast. The sudden catch in her breathing had nothing—nothing!—whatsoever to do with the fact that he had just pressed close beside her again.

"Did you find something?" His voice sounded near her ear.

She straightened, pulling away. "No. Not yet, at least." She put several feet between them by the simple expedient of examining the other side of the hearth.

"Now, why would I have been willing to wager you would not give up?" His smile held only teasing, no trace of any awareness of her as anything other than his childhood friend.

Which was exactly the way she wanted it. If she experienced any sensations of longing, it was only for days long gone, when Oliver would have been there with them. Abruptly she turned away. "If she wanted us to find something here, the least she could do would be to put in an appearance and show us what she had in mind."

"Very neglectful of her," he agreed. He looked once more around the room, then crossed to the far end, studying that wall as well.

His mother, who had followed them inside, rose from the chair she had taken. "I fail to see what she could possibly want in here."

"Or anywhere, for that matter." Tony ran a hand along the wainscotting, then shook his head. "If I hadn't seen her for myself, I would be inclined to think you were making a May game of me, Callie."

"I think it is she who is making one of both of us." Callie stifled a yawn. "Why do we not resume our search in the daylight? Perhaps we might see something we're missing with only the candles for illumination."

The other two agreed with this suggestion, and they trooped from the room back to the Blue Salon. There they found Marianne sitting in front of the tea tray, with the stoic Durstan standing guard at her side.

She looked up quickly, eyes wide. "Did you find something? No? Thank you, Durstan," she added as the butler beat a hasty retreat. "Poor man, he must have thought I was mad, but I simply could not stay in here alone, not when you had seen a ghost." She shivered.

"Where's Felix?" Tony asked.

Marianne hunched a shoulder. "He said he was going to bed. Except he carried the decanter of brandy with him. Will you take tea?"

This they did, with Callie sitting once more facing the mirror, her intent gaze never wavering from the reflective surface. What did Anne want of her? The thought kept repeating through her mind, over and over, bringing no new insights. At last, hoping for the oblivion of sleep, she rose, said her good nights, and started for the stairs. To her surprise, Marianne hurried from the room in her wake and fell into step beside her as they retrieved their chambersticks from the hall table.

"It's silly," Marianne said in a very small voice, "but I don't want to go up alone."

"It's not silly at all," Callie lied. "Though why Anne should start to bother you now, when you have lived in the same house with her for more than a year—"

Marianne gave an expressive shiver. "But I had never seen her before!"

"Then you may be sure she doesn't want anything from you." Callie started up the steps.

Marianne followed. "I'm glad you are here," she said after a moment. "When I first learned Tony planned to marry you, I was dreadfully upset, for you must know I wished him to marry an heiress. But now I am quite glad for him, for I see how very well you are suited. And that is of the utmost importance in a marriage."

"Well suited?" A shaky laugh escaped Callie. "Why, we fight like cats and dogs!"

Marianne nodded. "That is exactly what I mean, for only see how well the cats and Harold get on in this house."

Callie halted and stared at Marianne, her mind reeling. With an effort, she resumed her climb up the steps. Youthful adorations didn't last, she reminded herself. People grew up. They changed. Only memories remained, though they could sometimes trick a person into believing old feelings still lingered.

They reached the hall, but instead of heading toward the wing in which her own room lay, Marianne took a step after Callie, then hesitated. Callie pulled herself from her thoughts and regarded the other girl. A widow at age nineteen. Cause enough for anyone to look so unhappy. Only she didn't mourn her husband. Remembering Reginald, Callie couldn't blame her.

On impulse, Callie smiled. "Will you come to my room for a quiet coze? We have not had a chance yet to get to know one another."

Marianne brightened. "Oh, I should like it of all—" She broke off, a wariness damping her eagerness. "That is, do you think the ghost might come, too?"

"I have no idea," Callie admitted. "But I promise, I shall defend you if Anne should pay us a visit. Here," she scooped up the gray cat which now curled in the chair at the top of the stairs. "Let us bring Percival here with us. If Anne should appear, he'll alert us at once." She proceeded along the corridor, with the cat trying industriously to rub its face on her chin.

Partially reassured, Marianne followed her into the spacious chamber. She settled in a chair, where her wary gaze drifted to the fireplace which burned with gratifying warmth. Shadows filled the room, but nothing more. No ghostly flame flickered in welcome.

Callie curled onto the foot of the bed with Percy in her lap. "Are you in love with Felix?" she asked, blunt as always.

Marianne flushed. "Pray, do not be ridiculous. Felix despises me." Her fingers tugged at a bunch of ribands at her high waist.

Callie tilted her head to one side, watching the misery that seeped across the other girl's countenance. "He looks to me more like a gentleman keeping a prudent distance."

Marianne shook her head. "It would be impossible, even if he *did* care for me. Which he doesn't, of course. I have no money, and neither does he. My mama and my brother would never approve. And you know Felix," she went on, turning her misty regard on Callie. "Do you think he could ever be happy in any profession other than gaming?"

Callie only needed to consider a moment.

"No. He most definitely would not. The only solution will be for you to run away with him."

"Run—" Marianne stared at her, aghast. "Even if he did wish me to—which I assure you, he does not!—I would only be a burden to him. If he already owned a gaming establishment, that might be a different matter. But he does not, and has no hope of winning enough to start one, and—and this is the most ridiculous speculation! One must have money, for it is dreadful never being able to pay one's bills."

"It certainly is," Callie agreed with feeling. "But contracting a marriage not to one's liking would be even worse."

Ready tears brimmed in Marianne's eyes. "Oh, it is. So very dreadful. And I am so very glad for you, for you love Tony, and indeed, he will be the most excellent husband." She fished her handkerchief from her reticule and dabbed at her eyes. "What a joy it is to have you here. It is such a relief to have someone to talk to, who quite enters into my feelings." With that, she bid Callie a tremulous good night and sought her own room.

Callie stared after her. Love Tony? Well, of course she did, though not in the romantic sense Marianne implied. That idea was nonsense, and thinking about it a waste of time. She'd be far better employed trying to discover some solution to Marianne's seemingly insoluble dilemma with Felix. With that intent firmly in mind, she prepared for bed. But it was the image of Tony, once more young and whole, carefree and adventurous, that haunted her as she drifted off to sleep.

Some hours later, she awoke abruptly to a room steeped in darkness except for the glowing embers in the hearth. Silence filled the chamber, waiting, still, like someone holding their breath. Realizing that she did, Callie let it out, then drew in another deep one. Nothing . . .

She shivered with a sudden chill. From beside the hearth, a flame flickered, then advanced into the room. As she watched, the fire flared, became translucent, then shimmered into a vaguely human form. The hazy figure of Anne drifted forward, the ghostly flame still burning between her hands. For a long moment she paused at the foot of the bed, facing Callie, then she turned and vanished through the closed door.

Not that again. Would she ever be fast enough to see where the specter went next? Callie flung back the covers and dove after her, pausing only to open the door. This time she mustn't—couldn't!—be too late.

The glow of the wall sconces illuminated the corridor. Callie blinked in the light, alone, defeated once more. But not without a fight, she determined. With a muttered oath, she started down the hallway, willing Anne to reappear.

And there, on the Grand Staircase, she glimpsed the flickering of a flame that did not belong to any candle or oil lamp. She broke into a run, covering the distance in mere seconds. The ghostly light continued its descent, and Callie stumbled after it, clinging to the banister to keep from falling in her haste, wincing at the savage creaks of the ancient wood.

In the Great Hall, Anne moved to the right, along the corridor they took every evening after dinner. The Blue Salon. Without a doubt, Callie knew the destination. She reached the bottom stair and raced after the flame, just in time to see it coalesce once more into the figure of Anne as it drifted through the door of the salon.

Callie reached it moments later, flung it wide and rushed inside. Nothing. Complete blackness. Not even moonlight streamed through the drawn curtains. Frustrated, she looked about, then spotted a misty figure, barely discernible in the dark. It drifted toward the hearth, then faded into the mirror next to it. The hazy face of Anne turned back, stared for several seconds at Callie, then faded into nothingness.

Tony stirred in his bed, aware that some sound had disturbed his troubled sleep. He lay in silence, listening, and it came again: the creak of the stairs. Someone was about. Not the servants, for they'd use the back stairs. And this had to be someone unfamiliar with the steps, who didn't know which ones to avoid for stealth.

He swung out of his bed, found his dressing gown, and knotted the sash about his waist as he headed for the door. He reached the top of the staircase in time to see a ghostly shape in filmy white muslin exiting the Great Hall and running down a corridor. He set off in pursuit, his greater experience enabling him to move in near silence.

He found no difficulty in following his culprit; the door to the Blue Salon stood wide. He looked in to see Callie, wearing only a delicate nightdress, her thick braid of soft brown hair falling almost to her waist. She knelt at the hearth, struggling in determined silence to rekindle the blaze. As he watched, the tinder caught and tiny flames flared upward to caress the slender sticks waiting to receive them. From this, she lit a taper and set it into the stick that waited on the mantel. Light from the hearth erupted behind her, silhouetting her slight figure.

No, not so slight—at least not in some very notable areas. What, he wondered, had become of the little girl he had teased and argued with? How could she have grown into such a vision of grace and—and allurement. He stumbled over the word, rejecting it at first, then coming back to it as the only possible one to describe her. The filmy nightrail that wrapped about her entrancing form revealed as much as it concealed. The result played havoc with his mind.

Desire filled him, leaving him shaken with its intensity—and its inappropriateness. One didn't feel something like this for a girl one had known practically since her cradle. Or was that, in fact, what bothered him? Did he really feel that a lady so lovely, so alluring that any man must want to possess her, deserved better than him? She should have a husband who would take her to balls, dance with her, make her aware of what a precious treasure she was. Instead, he'd saddled her with the ruined shell of a man.

She turned then, started at sight of him, then gave her head a rueful shake, sending the escaping tendrils of dusky hair wisping about her cheeks. "You startled me," she said in a hoarse whisper.

"Sorry." He came forward. "I came to see who was about."

"Anne." She eyed him in sudden concern. "You look troubled. What's wrong?"

He shook his head. "Nothing that need concern you. Tell me what happened." She complied, and it both relieved and annoyed him that she didn't pursue the matter of what weighed on his mind. Probably, she didn't care; the only one whose troubles concerned her at the moment was Anne.

"We must have overlooked something obvious," she finished. She returned to the mirror beside the hearth and once more ran her fingers along every boss and carving of the wainscotting.

Tony remained where he stood, irrationally irritated with both Callie and the ghost. He had troubles, too. Why didn't she rally about him like she did about Anne? And why did she expect him to help a ghost, who'd been hanging about for a century, when he had more immediate disasters on his hands?

"You're not looking," she protested, and came to him, catching his hand to pull him into the room.

It felt soft in his, and as tiny as it was insistent. She drew him toward the hearth, but his concentration remained focused on her hand clasping his. Reluctantly, he forced his attention once more on the search, directing his thoughts to every irregularity the paneled wall boasted. In both respects, it proved to be of no avail: he found nothing; and his thoughts centered on Callie, so oblivious to him as she labored at his side.

At last, she stood back, frowning. "There must be something here." She gave an embossed pineapple a last tug and sighed when nothing happened.

"Well, if we're going to find it, Anne is going to have to stop beckoning and start pointing." Tony looked down at the tantalizing figure at his side, and fought back an urge to slide an arm about her shoulders and draw her close. She'd fit quite comfortably against him, her head just reaching the hollow of his shoulder. Which would put her waving curls in the perfect position for him to kiss them.

Abruptly, he turned toward the door. "Why don't we try to get some sleep? Maybe Anne will appear to you in a dream and tell us what to do next."

But as they headed up the stairs together, he found his thoughts dwelling not on his own bed, but on hers. With an effort, he fought off the vision of her lying beside him, soft, warm, and as eager to embrace him as she was to embrace life. To be with her would be to feel himself a whole man once more.

But he was beneath contempt to even consider such a thing for a moment. What he wanted and what Callie deserved were two very different things. If only he had sufficient money, he could break this sham betrothal, send her away while he still had the willpower to do what was right. If she remained near, temptation might well prove too strong.

Eight

Tony awoke early, but lay in his bed, reluctant to get up and face the morning. Callie also rose betimes, and he had no desire to sit tête-à-tête with her at the breakfast table. Better to wait until the others would be there, as well. Yet lying idle had never been easy for him. He compromised by dressing and making his way to the estate room, where he spent a fruitless hour reviewing which fields would be harvested first and trying to keep the vision out of his mind of Callie in that filmy night thing, her long braid tumbled across her shoulder.

Hunger at last drove him to seek the breakfast parlor, where the first sound to reach him was her laughter. He stopped dead, letting the warm, easy sound roll over him, and fought the longing to respond to its unspoken invitation to join in. He entered the apartment to find her sitting at the table, with Felix lounging at her side. Marianne sat opposite, her gaze fixed on her plate. His mother occupied the position of honor at the head of the table, from where she regarded Felix with the mixture of amusement and disapprobation that so often was directed toward him.

Callie looked up at his entry, studied his face in thoughtful silence for a moment, then announced: "I have decided to expand my search."

That brought him to a halt. "Have you?" he asked with considerable suspicion.

Visibly, her hackles rose, then subsided. "You needn't look like that. Trying to follow Anne has gotten us nowhere. I thought I might refamiliarize myself with the grounds, explore the stables to see if there are any relics in the carriage house that might provide any information about her."

"What an exciting morning you have planned," he drawled. And one in which he might well find himself enmeshed, when he wished to be anywhere except in her company. "But I fear," he added as he made his way to the sideboard and began to fill a plate, "you must hold me excused. I have business to which I must attend."

"It does sound like a delightful plan," ventured Marianne, hesitant but hopeful. "Such a pleasant morning to stroll about the grounds, too."

Felix groped at his waistcoat for his quizzing glass and leveled it at Marianne. "Can it be that you and I actually agree about something?" he marveled. "No, I must be mistaken. The mere thought is impossible. Callie, my dear, do you desire an escort? I find myself at loose ends this morning, and should be only too delighted to accompany you."

"Felix," said Lady Agatha at her most quelling, "you will oblige me by behaving yourself."

He dropped the glass and regarded her with mock puzzlement. "But my dear Cousin Agatha, surely I am doing precisely that. I have just pledged myself as escort and protector to Callie. What could possibly be wrong with such a plan?"

"Nothing in the least," Callie said quickly. "I should like it of all things if you would come with me, Felix. Shall we begin at once? Lady Lambeth?" She glanced at Marianne.

Marianne studied her plate. "I believe I have some chores I had forgotten. Pray, go without me."

"Your wish is my command." Felix directed an elegant leg at Marianne. Slipping his arm through Callie's, he drew her from the room.

Tony stabbed an unoffending chunk of ham and thrust it onto his plate, then decided he wasn't hungry after all. A mug of ale would be more to his taste. He poured this and steadfastly ignored the soft sound of Callie's laughter as she and Felix disappeared down the hall.

This was not, he told himself savagely, his idea of a quiet time in which to pull the estate back together. Damn Felix for being an impossible, capricious jackanapes! Yet to do him justice, how could any man help but be captivated by Callie's laughter and joy in life? Or did she enjoy life so much because she blossomed under Felix's attentions? That last thought disturbed him. Yet the possibility that he could be jealous, and of Felix of all people, he found ludicrous.

Irritated, he returned to the estate office, but found he had left nothing that needed his attention. The harvest had begun; there was little he could do but drive his curricle to the home farm and watch. But going to the stable meant a chance of encountering Callie.

Against his will, his steps led him to where he felt certain he would find her. He heard Felix's voice first, followed at once by Callie's joking rejoinder. He turned into the carriage house, and found them strolling arm in arm from one ancient vehicle to the next.

Felix looked up and hailed him. "What the deuce do you mean by storing all these wrecks?" he demanded with a gaiety at jarring odds with Tony's mood. "Only fit for the rubbish heap, the most of them."

"I feel certain there's one back here that Anne must have ridden in," Callie added.

"Did you sense her presence?" Tony reached them and paused, resting his aching leg.

"No." Callie shook her head in regret. "I don't think she's anywhere around."

"Undoubtedly she housed a horse or two through here." Tony offered her his arm, and she took it without any constraint. Which only went to show she regarded him as her old playmate. Vexed, he drew her onward, toward the stalls where the horses could be heard moving about in their straw, and the grooms went about their chores with cheerful disregard for the invasion of a party of ghost hunters.

Felix fell into step with them, grinning. "Do you know, Tony, if you will take over escorting Callie, I have some letters I need to write. Not, of course, that escorting you could be anything other than a delight," he added to Callie.

"Faint heart," she accused. "You just don't want to go tramping through the woods with me."

He sighed and shook his head. "It would quite take the polish off my boots, I fear. Tony, don't keep her out long, or I will have your mother demanding that I go in search of you." With an airy wave, he headed back toward the house.

"Incurably lazy," Callie remarked with a smile as she watched his departure, then turned back to Tony. "Are you going to show me that yearling I see over there? He seems to have good, sloping shoulders."

They passed some little time in the serious discussion of horseflesh, then strolled out toward the rose garden. One reminiscence led naturally into another, and he found the situation to be less strained than he'd anticipated. For minutes at a stretch he would slip easily back through time, only to be jarred once more into the present and the reminder that not a child, but a desirable young woman, walked at his side. The effect was heady.

The day was warm, and the sky directly above them a brilliant blue despite the thickening clouds that lingered on the horizon. Swans swam on the small lake, and the folly beckoned. They strolled toward it, stopping frequently for Callie to examine some prospect, or to point out some site of their youthful exploits, until it dawned on him that at this pace, he could walk a great deal farther than he would have expected. Pleased by this discovery, he found his depression lifting.

Callie paused by a bench and stared across the lake, in the direction of the home farm that lay beyond the line of yew trees in the distance. "How far will they get with the harvest today?"

He leaned against the wooden back, resting his leg. "A good portion of the first field, I hope. I'll drive out in a little while to see how it goes on."

"Will it be enough? To make the repairs, I mean?"

"The worst of them," he confirmed. "As long as the weather holds." He glanced automatically toward the horizon, but the clouds seemed content to keep their distance, for the moment at least. As they continued on their way toward the shrubbery maze, he added: "With luck, we'll have the roofs mended and the walls repaired before the rains set in."

"I haven't seen the farms, but if they are anything like the stable, I can only pity your poor tenants! I heard your mama speaking to the housekeeper about extra linens and blankets, and preserving extra vegetables in case of emergencies. No, I won't say a word about Reginald, but it is the outside of enough that the Grange should have been brought to such a state."

The intensity of this speech charmed him, and an overwhelming desire flooded over him to show his appreciation by kissing her. Oh, the devil, he just wanted to kiss her. Yet if he tried, would she reject his advances with revulsion— or merely with playful dismay? Or worse, would she submit to him as one bound by the duty of their betrothal?

The temptation to put it to the test proved strong enough to overcome his fear of rejection. He reached for her, and a sudden, wary expression lit her eyes. Incredibly, she swayed toward him, then as abruptly, she froze.

"Tony!" The sound was more a gasp than a cry.

He withdrew at once, embarrassed, disgusted with himself. Well, he had learned.

"Did you see it?" Still that same, hissing whisper.

Oh, he'd seen it all right, seen the rejection— Only she wasn't looking at him, but beyond his shoulder. Uncertain, he turned in time to see an odd light, in the middle of a hazy shape, moving along the hedge leading toward the maze.

"Anne? Out here?" His brain didn't seem to be working. Had Callie reacted to seeing Anne rather than to the realization that he intended to kiss her?

"I saw the flicker, then the movement—" Callie broke off.

Her fingers clutched his forearm, he realized. Gently, tentatively, he covered them with his hand. They were cold. "What?" He forced a rallying note into his voice. "Since when has Anne made you nervous?"

She hesitated a moment before answering, and when she spoke, her voice sounded abnormally subdued. "It's not Anne."

"Not—" He stared at her. "Callie, we've only got the one ghost haunting the Grange."

She gazed back, unblinking. "It wasn't Anne. Believe me, I've seen her enough in the past couple of days. It felt wrong."

"Dangerous?" He moved closer, his arm encircling her shoulder in a protective gesture.

She frowned, but made no attempt to escape his touch. "No," she said at last. "Not dangerous. Just not Anne."

"Then maybe we'd better have a look." Grasping her hand, he hurried as fast as his leg would permit to the spot he'd last seen the ghostly light that was apparently not his familiar specter. No trace of it lingered along the high hedge. Intrigued, he followed in the direction he had glimpsed it moving, toward the maze. Callie came willingly, but clinging to him.

A second ghost. The idea fascinated him, exhilarated him. Or was it the tangible, physical contact with Callie that sent his blood racing? He fought an impulse to swing her off her feet, into his arms. If he didn't approach this new aspect of their friendship with caution, he was like to receive a stinging rebuff—and caustic lecture—from her. And he would much rather receive something very different.

"Did you see that?" Callie whispered from very close at his side.

"No." In fact, only half his mind had been occupied with the search. The rest remained focused on the slender, vital girl at his side.

"I thought I caught a glimpse of light. In there." She pointed through the opening of the maze.

He flashed her a grin, his spirits soaring with the enjoyment of the chase—and of her company. "Only one way to find out." Together, they started in. No need to lead the way, or even remind Callie of the key; she must know it almost as well as he.

It didn't take long to negotiate, not since they knew which paths to tread, and in only a few minutes they emerged into the rectangular center. Before them, a fountain stood in the middle of a reflecting pool, both dry. Stone benches flanked this on either side, and behind it stood a tiny Grecian temple. It had been some time since he'd come here, he realized, looking at the trailing spiderwebs and the weeds that had erupted through the moss that separated the paving stones of the path.

Callie's fingers tightened their grip on him, and she shivered. "Doesn't anyone come here anymore?" she asked, echoing his own thoughts.

"From the looks of it, not even the undergroom. I'll set someone to—no, there'll be no one to spare until after the harvest."

She squeezed his hand. "Never mind. You can set it to rights later." She stood for a long moment, then shook her head. "I feel something, but I don't see anything. Whoever it is, she—or he—is hiding." Abruptly, she released her hold on him. "Why can't your ghosts do something other than just lead us on these ridiculous chases? If they want something, the least they could do would be to make it clear!"

"I suppose you think I should have a talk with them?"

"Well, they're your family ghosts, aren't they?"

"Anne, yes. I have no idea who this one is."

Callie tilted her head to one side. "Perhaps your mama will know."

Tony took her arm and started back toward the entrance. "If she doesn't, she'll probably inform it that it has no business here and order it to move out." They made the first turning, and a sudden, icy chill gripped him. He spun to look back, but could make out nothing.

In silent agreement, they returned to the house, heading toward the library doors which stood ajar. They mounted the steps to the tiled terrace, but as they approached the curtained opening, Felix's voice reached them. Callie hesitated.

In an unaccustomed, savage tone, Felix declared: "There's no hope for you but to marry a wealthy man like your mama wants. It's all you're suited for, to decorate your husband's table."

"You are cruel!" cried Marianne. "And completely unjust. I have no desire to wed anyone! Anyone at all! Least of all a self-centered Captain Sharp like you, who cares for nothing but the throw of the dice or the turn of the cards, or the—the fleecing of poor pigeons!" Soft footsteps ran across the carpet, and the slamming of the inner door announced her departure.

Tony held a finger to his lips, and Callie nodded. Together they retreated a few paces and allowed a couple of minutes to pass.

"You should have brought your shawl," Tony announced in a voice guaranteed to carry to any occupant in the room beyond.

"But it was quite warm when we set out," Callie protested, playing along as he'd known she would. "And I am not in the least chilled now, though you will make such a dreadful fuss." She shot him a teasing look.

"I? Fuss? When it is you who are forever finding fault?" He drew the drapes back for her to pass in before him. It took a moment for his eyes to adjust to the sudden darkness; then he saw Felix sprawled on a couch, fighting off the advances of the black and white Archimedes. "Ah, there you are, Felix. I thought you'd be long finished with your letters, by now. What are you still doing inside on such a pleasant day?"

"Attempting to convince this benighted animal that I have no desire to be covered in cat hairs." He looked up, his face drawn despite the determined smile that seemed pasted on his mouth. "How has your search progressed?"

"What would you say," Callie asked, eyes gleaming, "if we were to tell you there are not one, but two ghosts haunting Lambeth Grange?"

"I'd say I'd pack my things upon the instant. You're not serious, are you?" he added with suspicion born of a long acquaintance with Callie.

"Very serious." Quickly, she summed up the events in the maze. "And you cannot leave, for we quite count on you to help us."

"Good gad," he said when she'd finished. He looked toward Tony. "It's Callie, you know. Trouble follows her."

Tony shook his head. "Actually, it races to meet her!"

* * *

Callie curled onto the sofa in the Blue Salon that evening, staring pensively into the blazing hearth. Beside it, the aged Harold dozed, toes twitching with canine dreams. Percival stretched in her lap, flexed his claws, then closed his eyes as she absently rubbed his chin. Already, gray cat hairs clung to the amber crepe of her gown.

Two ghosts. And Tony blamed *her.* It was his house—as she'd pointed out to him. Therefore they must be his ghosts. He'd merely shaken his head in mock sadness, reminded her the spectral activity had increased significantly only since she had come to stay, and left her to seethe.

Lady Agatha had been unable to enlighten her as to the possible identity of their second specter. And, as her undutiful son had predicted, she had taken its presence as a personal affront. She declined to join in Callie's speculations about why it had chosen to appear in the maze that day, and other than animadverting upon the apparent tendency of every specter in the neighborhood to drop in uninvited, had little to say on the subject.

A soft exclamation from Marianne caused Callie to glance across to where the girl sat in a chair, buried in the pages of the latest issue of *La Belle Assemblee.* Her rapt expression made it obvious that no otherworldly intrusion, but some cunningly designed gown, had caused her outburst. Callie glanced over her shoulder to where Lady Agatha and Felix argued amicably over their game of piquet, then turned her attention to the box of letters that rested at her side.

Tony, in the other chair, already leafed through a bundle, checking the dates and laying them aside. That second ghost had worried Tony, she reflected. He'd seemed withdrawn since they'd seen it.

Which was as well, perhaps. The oddest sensation had come over her as they'd strolled through the shrubbery. She'd felt breathless, nervous, and very much aware of him at her side. When he'd taken her hand in his, her heart had pounded so hard she'd been surprised he hadn't heard it. And she'd thought of little else ever since. She considered each symptom, and came to the dismayed conclusion that childhood infatuations could, in fact, be rekindled.

Or was it merely an infatuation? She studied his intent face, her gaze traveling over every familiar angle and plane. She'd always loved him, she supposed. For his daring, his laughter, his teasing, his intensity, and innate kindness to her. She'd loved him, but always known he was not for her. So she'd tried to close him out of her heart and think of him only as a friend.

But the years hadn't changed anything. She still loved him—and he still wasn't for her.

Oh, he'd offered for her, but out of desperation, both to see her taken care of and to free himself from facing any other, more critical female. She'd seemed safe to him. But he would recover, and long for London. And when he went, he'd meet the Season's reigning Incomparable, and regret tying himself to Oliver's little sister with the volatile temper.

The best possible thing she could do for him would be to refuse to marry him. But she could hardly reject him before he'd built up his confidence in himself once again. Which meant that any number of weeks still lay ahead, where she'd have to see him daily, at considerable pain to herself. Well, she'd have to help him heal as quickly as possible.

Heal, so he could leave her and find some other, more suitable lady.

It was not a pleasant reflection, but she knew she would do anything for Tony. Teasing helped him. So did arguing with him. And so did encouraging him to help Anne.

Involuntarily, her gaze shifted to the mirror, where she had twice before seen the ghostly image. And there, deep within the glass, she glimpsed the flickering of that unearthly flame. It moved forward, into the room, then seemed to skim along the floor.

"The floor." Without realizing it, she spoke the words aloud.

Tony looked up. "The what?"

She stared at him for a long moment, the blinding simplicity of her realization leaving her stunned. "The floor," she repeated. "We've checked the wall, but not the floor!" Even as she spoke, she sprang to her feet, dislodging the outraged Archy and scattering the papers she'd held. In four running steps she reached the mirror, and knelt at the baseboard beneath.

Just below the gilt-framed glass, nearly three feet from the hearth, her fingers found an irregularity in the wood, not quite a knothole, yet not perfectly smooth. She pressed it.

With a creak of aging hinges, a panel in the wall slid sideways.

Nine

Callie fell back, too startled to catch herself. Behind her, Marianne gave a soft shriek, and the others jumped from their chairs.

"Merciful heavens!" breathed Lady Agatha. "A priest's hole!"

"Oh!" chimed in Marianne's tremulous voice. "Oh, how dreadful!"

The musty smell of the ages washed over Callie as she scrambled to her feet. Tony caught her arm and helped her to rise, but he did so absently, his attention focused on the darkness of the narrow cavity that yawned before them.

"You found it," he breathed. "Callie, you found it!" He ended on a laugh of triumph as he swung her from her feet, spinning her about. As he set her down, he kissed her, soundly but without passion, then turned to join the others as they crowded about their discovery.

Callie staggered back a step, shaken. That kiss had meant nothing to him, just the exuberance of the moment. Yet her entire world had shattered, only to refigure itself in new and incredible forms, with him as its center. More fool she.

But she wasn't a fool, and nor was she one to give up something she wanted without a fight. He might think of her as nothing more than a convenience at the moment, but she would see to it that changed. He would learn. What, exactly, she wasn't sure. She only knew that she must bring him to love her as she loved him, and she only had until his spirit began to heal.

Suddenly, the time that moments before had loomed before her like an endless stretch of days, now threatened to sift as quickly as sand between her grasping fingers.

The babble of voices about her roused her from her brooding reflections. She looked up, guiltily aware that her attention had been elsewhere. Yet under the circumstances, she felt she had some excuse.

"It is for Calpurnia to do, do you not think, Felix?" Lady Agatha protested in a voice of admonition.

"By all means," said Tony. "She has certainly earned the right."

"Then why doesn't she get on with it?" Felix grumbled. "Callie, my dear, you see us breathless with anticipation. Pray do not hold us in suspense a moment longer!"

"But do you want to, Miss Rycroft?" Marianne shivered. "I vow, I could not bear to go in there."

"Nonsense!" Felix directed a scathing look at the girl. "Callie is up to anything. Aren't you?"

Callie rallied. "Of a certainty." She stepped forward, for the first time actually looking at what she had labored so hard to uncover.

The entryway was small, barely four feet tall and less than three feet wide. By the light of the branch of candles Felix held, she could make out the meager contents of the cupboard beyond. A small drop-front writing desk, perched on twist legs, practically filled the area. A three-branched candelabrum stood on its narrow top. Before it stood a scrolled walnut Charles II high-backed chair. Nothing else met her searching gaze.

Callie hesitated; the chill that emanated from that tiny room came from no earthly source. Anne hovered nearby. And Anne waited for Callie to enter, to find whatever secret had been hidden here for a hundred years.

She could hardly blame the poor ghost for growing impatient. "A candle, Felix?" She held out her hand for the taper Felix extracted from the holder.

"Are you sure you should?" asked Marianne in a quavering voice.

"I'm positive." With that, Callie ducked through the low opening and entered the priest's hole.

The others crowded near the entrance, watching; there wouldn't be room for any of them to join her. Quickly, she lit the candles that had stood there for forgotten ages; they sprang to life, filling the room with a dancing, comforting light, dispelling the mustiness. A fourth flame danced among them: Anne, taking an active interest. Callie's heart beat faster.

A muffled shriek escaped Marianne. "She— she's there! The ghost!" The girl spun away, encountered Felix's shoulder, and clung to him.

Felix, still clutching the candelabrum, caught Marianne to him with his free arm. "She'll not harm you," he assured her, forgetting for once to be disagreeable about it.

Gingerly, Callie drew out the chair and sat in it. It neither creaked nor gave way, but supported her comfortably. That fear satisfied, she turned her attention to the desk. Three drawers ranged across the front, below the slanted panel that would lower to form the writing surface. She ran her fingers along the drawer on the left, then pulled it open. The ghostly flame burned brighter, and Callie realized she held her breath. She forced it out in a long sigh.

Nestled inside lay a number of yellowed letters bound together with a pink riband. A delicate scent of roses wafted from them; someone had scattered around the sheets several dried blossoms, which had crumbled now to fragments and dust. Yet even after all these years, the aroma persisted. With hands that trembled, Callie lifted the precious discovery from its hiding place and turned to the others.

Tony took the bundle from her, his smile a caress. "You've done it," he said softly.

"Do you think so? Do you suppose this is what Anne wants? For us to read these?"

"You may have the privilege. As tempting as they may be, we won't touch them until you're done in there."

"Get on with it!" Lady Agatha crowded close,

her gaze resting on the letters. "Hurry and finish with the desk so you can read these."

Obediently, Callie returned to her task. The second drawer contained nothing except a yellowed linen handkerchief with the initial *A* embroidered in elegant filigree in one corner. Callie laid it back in its resting place and opened the third drawer. Another handkerchief lay within, with dried and discolored roses pressed between its every fold. They must once have boasted every color, for tinges of pink, red, yellow, and white remained. She lifted it out carefully, only to reveal more of the same delicate muslin squares beneath.

"Is there a tray?" she asked, and looked over her shoulder.

Marianne, who stood in silence beside Felix, hurried to a pier table against the other wall. On this stood a silver salver beside a matching candlestick. With tender hands, she carried her find back to the others, then came to an abrupt halt several feet from the opening into the priest's hole.

"What? Afraid of an old desk?" Felix, back in his usual form, regarded her with a curling lip. "Faint heart." He took the salver from her and handed it, with all due ceremony, to Callie.

One by one, she deposited the floral-laced handkerchiefs onto the tray. That something lay beneath them, she felt certain. What it might be she had no clue, but the building of anticipation made it impossible to draw a normal breath. The ghostly flame flickered near her hand, as if urging her to work faster. Yet she didn't dare, for fear of damaging whatever treasure might lie hidden.

She removed more crumbled petals, only to have her fingers brush the bottom of the drawer. Surprised, she hurriedly removed the last remnants. Nothing. Absolutely nothing lay beneath. Yet she would have sworn that here she would have found the most important artifact of all. Disbelieving, she peered within, holding the candelabrum to give herself the maximum amount of illumination, but to no avail. Nothing.

"What is it?" Tony leaned over her shoulder, watching.

She shook her head. "Just a nonsensical notion, I suppose. I had the oddest sensation—but never mind, it hardly matters. The roses must have been of great importance to Anne."

With that, she eased the chair back a little and let down the top of the desk. Within lay a series of pigeonholes and narrow shelves, on which someone had stacked a selection of yellowed papers, wax, seals, quill pens, ink containers, and a pot of sand: all the elements necessary for the writing of letters. Callie rifled through the embossed sheets, finding nothing, then examined the seals. These she passed to Tony, then sat back, eyeing the desk with uncertainty.

Tony frowned. "Nothing more?"

"How much more do you want?" demanded Felix. "You've got a packet of letters. Aren't those enough?"

"And the lovely flowers," added Marianne. "How much she must have cared about them, to have preserved them so. Do you suppose they were the last ones given to her by her beloved Henry?"

"Before he betrayed her, you mean?" asked Felix. "She'd be more likely to cast them on the fire."

"Are we even certain this is Anne's desk?" stuck in Lady Agatha. "I should certainly not wish to do my letter writing in such a cramped and uncomfortable place."

"It implies some activity of a sinister nature," Felix breathed in sepulchral accents. "Do you suppose that in the dark of night, when no one else was astir, she would creep down here to her secret room for some fell purpose?"

Marianne shivered. "Pray, do not," she begged.

"If she did anything in secret, it would have been for the Jacobite cause," Tony said. "That was treasonous, and cause enough for secrecy."

"Yet her ghost has been so very urgent for us—for Calpurnia—to find this." Lady Agatha pressed closer, studying the back wall of the priest's hole. "Could there be something else concealed in there?"

"Aren't letters enough? How much do you want?" Felix demanded. "Or won't you be satisfied with anything less than a skeleton?"

"Do not even think such a dreadful thing!" Marianne protested.

Lady Agatha directed a quelling eye at her reprobate relative. "Do not be ridiculous, Felix, if you can possibly help it. Which I take leave to doubt. Anne's body was not hidden. It lies in the family crypt along with a number of our other ancestors. You may go and see if you wish, though you will only be able to read her name and the dates on which she was born and died."

Felix wrinkled a fastidious nose. "I'll take your word for it. But I believe I was referring to a metaphorical skeleton. Or do I mean a skeleton in the abstract?"

"Stop this talk of skeletons, I beg you!" Marianne shivered. "I vow, I shan't be able to sleep a wink tonight."

Felix's eyes gleamed. "It's not the skeletons you have to fear, you know. They're almost harmless compared to their ghosts and—"

"Felix!" Lady Agatha glowered at him. "If you cannot behave yourself, you may go to your room. I will not have Marianne distressed."

"What? Order me to my chamber? I am not a little boy of ten!" the malefactor protested.

"No," she agreed cordially. "Closer to eight, I should imagine, from your behavior. Calpurnia, if there is nothing else there, you will oblige me by reading those letters and satisfying our curiosity."

Thus called to order, Callie ducked out of the cupboardlike room, retrieved the letters from Tony, and carried them to the sofa. The spaniel, she noted, had retreated to the far side of the room, where he sprawled in a corner, watching them with his graying muzzle resting on his forepaws. Archimedes and Percival, on the other hand, sniffed with interest about the opening of the priest's hole.

Felix presented Callie with the branch of candles, then strolled to the table on which lay the decanters of brandy and negus. He poured himself a glass of the former, then settled in a chair to enjoy it. His gaze, though, rested on the letters Callie held.

With the distinct sensation that she intruded into where she had no business to venture, Callie untied the riband and lifted the first of the folded sheets. It bore the appearance of much handling, as if it had been read many times. Bracing herself for she knew not what, she began to read.

My beloved Anne, it began. She scanned to the bottom of the sheet and found the signature. *Yours always, your most obedient and adoring, Henry.* Henry's letters to Anne.

Were these what Anne wished found? It seemed odd, unless Anne wished for Callie to be confronted by the perfidy of her long-dead relative. She would have to read them all, she supposed, though she shrank from the task. She would rather burn them all than thrust herself into something so private and intimate as a *billet doux.* Yet it seemed that Anne herself wished them read. Callie made a silent vow to herself that, if given the chance before she died, she would burn any such letters she ever received.

That matter settled in her mind, she returned her attention to the first of the letters, and found herself drawn in by the depth of emotion. How could anyone who read these doubt the love expressed in every impassioned line? And how could any woman not long to be loved like that?

Involuntarily, her gaze strayed to where Tony now sat at the desk in the priest's hole. No, that line of thought would lead her nowhere. Besides, these letters contained nothing but lies. She had to repeat that fact to herself several times. They were lies, for Henry betrayed Anne.

"What do they say?" demanded Lady Agatha when Callie at last laid down the final one.

As she piled the letters neatly once more, Callie told her. She retied the riband about them, then held the missives tightly in both hands. "What a consummate scoundrel he must have been!" she declared. "To have courted her solely for her wealth! And she, poor soul, was utterly deceived."

"And then he hit upon the Jacobite scheme as a way of winning her fortune without burdening himself with a wife." Lady Agatha frowned. "Really, Calpurnia, one hates to speak ill of someone's relatives, but his behavior was inexcusable."

"And that was what Anne wanted me to know." Callie regarded the bundle in her hands with a pensive frown. "I cannot blame her. I only wish she'd show me some way I could make it up to her."

"Poor Anne," Marianne sighed. "Was he truly so convincing that she did not have the least inkling as to his true intentions?"

"If I did not know the truth," Callie said slowly, "I should be convinced he loved her more than life itself. No, he was utterly convincing."

"Her shock when she learned the truth, how

completely he had betrayed her—" Marianne broke off and hugged herself.

"She couldn't live with the pain," Felix ended for her, softly.

Callie stared at Felix's unaccustomed solemnity, but any pithy comments seemed inappropriate.

"Callie?" Tony called from where he sat at the desk in the priest's hole, his voice strained. He had pulled the third drawer, the one that had held the dried roses, free from the desk. It now rested in his lap. He didn't look at it, though. His gaze rested on the gaping hole it left.

Callie laid the letters aside and rose. "What is it?"

"There's a false back. Do you wish to open it?"

She'd been right. That drawer did hold something of more importance than the flowers, however carefully someone had preserved them. Every nerve tingled along the back of her neck, setting her shivering. She crossed to the low entryway, but experienced no desire to wedge herself into the tiny area. Instead, she knelt on the Aubusson carpet before it. After a moment, she said: "You found it. Go ahead, see if there's something there."

He needed no further urging. He reached inside, felt for a moment, then a soft exclamation of satisfaction escaped him. "There's a catch here. Yes, it's releasing something." He fumbled for a moment, then drew out a small plain box. He held it low so that Callie could watch as he opened it.

A folded paper lay within, yellowed as had been the others. He removed it, then spread and smoothed the sheet on the slanted surface of the writing desk. "It's a letter," he announced.

"Well, read it!" urged Felix. "Who wrote it? To whom is it addressed?"

Tony checked. "It's signed with an initial. A *C.* And it's addressed to someone called *Q.*"

"But what does it say?" demanded his mother.

Tony glanced down the closely written sheet, frowning. "Whoever they were, they seem to have been about some mischief of some sort," he said at last.

"What?" Felix dropped to one knee beside Callie. "If you won't hurry with it, man, then come out of there so we can read it over your shoulder!"

Tony complied, moving to stand before the hearth with the multibranched candelabrum at his back. His mother and Felix gathered about him, trying to see. Callie stood aside, watching his face, waiting.

"It doesn't say what they've done," he told Callie after another moment. "There's just a reference to the 'dreadful deed.'"

"It seems that our *C* has destroyed whatever evidence there may have been," Felix added. "Well, I must say, that wasn't very thoughtful of him, was it? How the devil are we to find out what they did?"

Lady Agatha regarded him with exaggerated patience. "That was probably the point. And you will kindly refrain from using such language in the presence of ladies."

"Whatever they did," Tony went on, ignoring his two relatives, "*C* says it has all been for naught. And he ends it by saying, 'May God have mercy upon our souls. We shall have need of it.' " He lowered the missive. "What do you make of that?"

"We might better be able to tell if we knew who *C* and *Q* were," Callie mused. "Do you have any idea? This could have been hidden in there for countless ages before Anne's time."

Tony shook his head. "It's dated the nineteenth of April, 1713. That's about the time Anne died."

Marianne, who had been sitting on a chair watching with wide eyes, paled. "Do you think they murdered her?"

"Don't be ridiculous." Felix regarded her with a pitying expression. "She killed herself."

Marianne straightened. "That was the story everyone was told. What if she had been *thrown* from that dreadful window instead?"

Lady Agatha stared at her. "It might be possible. Only why? Henry had already vanished with the money. *Q* and *C* couldn't have hoped to save it at that point."

Felix turned to stare at her. "Had he vanished with it? I mean, are you certain? Or could they have murdered our Anne to keep her from giving him the fortune?"

"No." Callie shook her head. "He absconded with the money. Remember, he took my family's fortune as well. If he hadn't made off with it, we would certainly know. He couldn't have—"

She broke off as a new and startling idea forced itself into her mind.

"They committed some foul deed," Felix declared, doggedly sticking to the one point of which he was certain. "And if it wasn't the murder of Anne, what could it have been?"

Callie's gaze shifted to the *billet-doux* tied with the pink riband. "It was Henry," she said with a certainty that surprised her. "They murdered Henry for the money. That was why he never came for his beloved Anne. He didn't betray her. He couldn't have—you'd know that if you'd read his letters. No, they stopped him from coming, and Anne never knew the truth."

"Good God," said Felix.

"It's possible." Lady Agatha went to the table and picked up Henry's letters, then looked back at Callie. "That would certainly put a different light on Anne's haunting us all these years."

"Who are *C* and *Q*?" asked Marianne. "Dreadful people, to be sure, but were they related to Anne?"

"Where is the Bible with the family tree?" Tony asked his mother.

"I saw it in the muniments room," said Callie. "I'll just be a moment."

She darted out the door and hurried through the corridors until she found herself outside the chamber where she'd spent an incredibly boring morning only a couple of days before. The Bible lay on the table inside. Flipping to the front, she found where generation upon generation of Lambeths had entered the records of births, marriages, and deaths in a variety of fists, from elegant to almost illegible. She ran her finger along the columns until she encountered the mention of Anne's death, then continued backward, looking for anyone with the initial of *C* or *Q*, either first or last name.

Felix strode into the room. "Did you find it?"

"I'm looking." She never raised her gaze from the page.

"Have you found them?" Lady Agatha followed him inside, with Marianne at her heels. Tony's uneven footsteps sounded in the corridor beyond.

"There's a Charles, but he seems to have been—" She broke off and calculated. "A great uncle. That's a possibility. Oh, dear, here's another Charles, his son. It could have been either of them, I suppose. Then there's a Cedric, who was her father's brother."

"Cedric," mused Lady Agatha. "His portrait is in the gallery upstairs. I believe he managed the estate for a number of years."

"Cedric it is, then," decided Felix. "What about *Q*?"

Callie looked up from the genealogy, sobered. "Anne's older half brother was named Quentin."

Felix let out a soft whistle. "The estate's owner and its manager. Probably always in need of more money, then they get wind that Anne is contemplating throwing her fortune to the wind in a traitorous cause. So they kill Henry, tell Anne he absconded, and keep the money for themselves. No wonder they felt their souls needed mercy."

"This is all conjecture," pointed out Tony,

who had joined them. "If you'll remember, the letter said their dreadful deed was all for naught."

"Could that be because Anne killed herself?" Marianne suggested. "It would be such a dreadful thing, for them to know they had driven her to suicide. It would have turned their seeming windfall to ashes."

"I suspect they were made of sterner stuff than that," drawled Felix. "If they got their hands on the Rycroft fortune, that would explain how the Lambeth family restored their finances."

"Except it took several generations to do that," Lady Agatha pointed out. "The family very definitely suffered at that time."

"And the letter said it was all for naught," Tony mused. "So *if* they murdered Henry, what became of the money?"

"I'm sure they did," said Callie, clinging to her conviction that sprang only from her reading of Henry's letters.

"You just don't want to believe your relative to have been such a rum touch." Felix shook his head. "You know, of course, none of this makes any sense?"

And with that, Callie reluctantly had to agree.

Ten

After a long moment of silence, Callie shook her head. "We need to know more. Tony, could there have been any other secret compartments in that desk?"

A reluctant smile tugged at his mouth. "How many startling revelations do you want? That priest's hole has already produced quite a bit."

"I know, but it's not enough. If there were any other pieces of information, do you not think they would have been hidden in there, along with the rest? We can't simply give up at this point. *Did* Quentin and Cedric murder Henry? If not, what was their dreadful deed? And if they did, what became of the money?"

"Not all questions can be answered." Lady Agatha studied the Bible over Callie's shoulder. "It might not have been Cedric, but one of the Charleses. There's a very great deal we don't know."

"But I want to know," Callie exclaimed.

"And you're not going to give up until you do, are you?" Warm amusement lit Tony's eyes. "Very well, I will search the desk again. Would you care to examine the walls for any other secret hiding places?"

"How absolutely delightful," drawled Felix. "I shall watch."

The prospect didn't delight Callie, either, but it offered the only chance of uncovering answers. They returned to the Blue Salon, where the door to the tiny chamber remained open. Callie slipped inside first, and set to work feeling the paneled walls for any secreted springs, levers or any other device that might reveal more clues to their mystery. Tony followed her within and settled once more at the writing desk. Lady Agatha and Marianne withdrew to chairs with the collection of Henry's letters. Felix made straight for the brandy decanter, then strolled over to watch the progress of the search.

Behind her, Callie could hear the scrapings as Tony pulled out each drawer to subject its cavity to a thorough examination. Several minutes passed before he spoke, and when he did, his voice rose on a note of excitement.

"Callie?"

"What have you got there?" Felix ducked down to peer inside; the priest's hole couldn't hold three people.

From within the opening for the drawer in which Callie had found the handkerchief, Tony drew out a wooden box of the same dimensions as the drawer, except barely more than two inches in height. Callie stopped work and turned to his side, waiting, breath held.

"It was concealed in the top, above the drawer. It fitted perfectly into the base of the desk area." He held it out to her. "Do you want the honor?"

She shook her head. "Go ahead."

"One of you go ahead!" Felix leaned closer.

"Pray, do not keep us in suspense," added Lady Agatha, who had positioned herself just behind Felix. "Do move over," she added to that gentleman. "You are quite blocking our view."

Tony slid the thin lid from the box. At first, it appeared as if only a crumpled handkerchief lay within. Then he touched it, revealing a long, flat object wrapped within the linen. He lifted it out and pulled the cloth away.

"A dagger!" exclaimed Callie.

"That's blood!" added Felix.

Startled, Callie stared at the brownish smears on the linen square. She took it from Tony, turning it in her hands to examine it. "There's an embroidered *A* in the corner, just like the other one," she announced.

"Then they did murder Anne instead of Henry," Felix said, sounding disappointed.

A soft moan from the room beyond was Marianne's only comment.

Tony turned the dagger in his hand. "There's something on this."

"Dried blood, probably," said Felix. "Lord, why didn't they clean the thing?"

"There's something still in the box." Callie pressed closer. "A paper."

Tony handed the dagger to Callie, who received it in the handkerchief, then extricated the single folded sheet from its resting place.

He spread it with care, then held it so Callie could read over his shoulder.

"*I, Cedric Lambeth,*" she read, deciphering the wavering script with some difficulty, "*am compelled by the burden that weighs upon my soul to make full confession for the evil that I have wrought this night.*"

"Well, that answers that." Felix nodded in satisfaction. "Cedric, not one of the Charleses."

"Do be quiet." Lady Agatha glared at him. "Go on, Calpurnia."

Callie shook her head. "You read it, Tony."

He glanced up at her, then skimmed the letter. "You were right about Henry, Callie. They did kill him. Quentin overheard Anne and Henry setting the time for their elopement with the family fortunes. They were bound for France, it seems, to join the Old Pretender and his followers. So when Henry came to meet Anne, they were waiting for him. Cedric says that without Henry's influence, they would be able to manage Anne. He had no idea when he wrote this that she would kill herself."

"Unless they couldn't manage her, and were forced to kill her, as well," Felix suggested.

"Are there any more secret drawers?" Callie asked Tony.

He shook his head. "Short of taking the desk apart piece by piece, of course, I cannot be certain. But I think I've found them all."

"Then I doubt they killed poor Anne—except by driving her to suicide. They would have left another confession."

"I am inclined to agree with that," said Lady Agatha. "Poor Anne."

"And this is what she wanted us to find," Callie said. "Henry's letters, and this. She wanted it known he never betrayed her."

"How romantic, and how terribly sad." Marianne brushed the moisture from her brimming eyes. "Imagine having a love like that, so fierce and wonderful, yet so tragic. A love that lasts beyond the grave."

Felix turned to stare at the girl, but before he could speak, Callie stomped down on the toe of his evening slipper and glared at him. He started, directed an outraged look at her, then comprehension spread across his features and he kept his tongue.

"And so ends our adventure," said Tony.

"Do you suppose Anne will stop haunting the Grange now?" Marianne asked. "I mean, now that the truth is known? Surely there's no longer any need for her to linger."

"You sound disappointed!" Felix accused. "I thought you were afraid of her."

"I am. That is, I'm not really *afraid* of her, it's just the thought of a ghost." She shivered. "And now that I know the true story, I don't think I'd mind her presence at all. Well, not too much, at least." She sighed. "Only think what a splendid gothic tale someone could write about her."

Callie leaned against the paneled wall, her gaze resting on Tony's pensive countenance. He looked from the confession to the dagger and back again. Another worry, Callie realized. Now that he knew the truth, he, too, wanted to make some confession about what truly occurred. But to what authorities could one report a murder that took place a hundred years before?

"The vicar, perhaps?" she suggested.

Tony looked up, startled out of his reverie. He thought for a moment, and the tension in his brow eased. "You are probably right. I believe I shall feel a great deal better once I have given these into his keeping. And I must say, it will be a considerable relief to have this matter settled. It's time I concentrated on the estate instead of Anne." He rose and stepped toward the low door opening, forcing the others to give way to allow him to exit.

And that, Callie reflected, was that. The fun and excitement of their mystery had come to an end, and Tony would once more immerse himself into worry.

She couldn't allow that. He might think he longed for peace and quiet, but she knew him far too well to believe he could ever be happy without laughter and enthusiasm. She could almost regret having settled Anne's affairs.

Tony seated himself on the sofa with a copy of the *London Times*. Harold padded over, circled three times, and heaved himself down on the floor with a heartfelt sigh. Archibald promptly claimed the position on Tony's lap, leaving Marmaduke to fend for himself.

Felix, Lady Agatha, and Marianne said their good nights and headed for their rooms. Callie, thoughtful, watched them go, then picked up Henry's letters once more. Yet her thoughts remained focused on Tony—and on herself.

He liked her well enough. He even, for some unheard of reason, enjoyed her ready temper and their frequent arguments. But that was a far cry from loving her. If nothing but dull days of worry stretched ahead of him, he would accept the unexciting as his lot in life. He would continue to regard her as a little sister, and he would still want to marry her simply because that was safer and easier than taking the risk of falling in love.

That wasn't enough for her. She wanted his love—which meant she would have to make him see her in a different light, wake him up to the fact that the best part of himself hadn't been destroyed on that battlefield. It would be a hard, uphill struggle for her, and so far Anne had been her best ally. Unless she could think of something to shake him to his very foundations, her hopes of love would be nothing but a ghost flame, a mere reflection of Anne's and Henry's romance.

Restless, she laid aside the letters and picked up Cedric's confession that lay on the desk beside the dagger, and read it all the way through. His expression of horror at what he had done might have moved her more had he not planned his brutal crime for so tawdry a motive as material wealth. *The hope of the fortune,* he wrote. Her distaste veered suddenly into uncertainty.

"Tony." She held her burgeoning excitement in check. "Cedric speaks of the *hope*. It sounds as if he never laid hands on it."

Tony looked up from the paper he leafed through. "What, aren't you willing to admit we've solved the mystery?"

"I'm not so sure we have. If he murdered

Henry for the fortune, then all that wealth Henry carried must have fallen into his hands."

Slowly, the *Times* lowered to Tony's lap. "Unless Henry wasn't carrying it." He held out his hand for the confession, and Callie took it to him, then knelt at his side to study it with him.

"Nowhere," Callie persisted, "does Cedric mention actually laying hold of the monies with which Henry and Anne intended to flee. You don't think his crime so revolted him that he renounced the cache, do you?"

"Not really," Tony admitted. "Even if he did, what did he do with it? My mama feels certain the Lambeth fortunes were not restored by it."

She nodded, her excitement bursting forth. "The Rycrofts never got it back, that much we know. So that means the monies must be somewhere. But where?"

Tony considered, frowning. "Do you think Cedric's remorse would have been as great had he obtained the fortune?"

"No." She felt certain of that. "Remember that bit in his letter to Quentin? About it all being for naught? He might have been able to buy off his conscience if their plot had worked."

"So if Cedric and Quentin never got it," Tony mused, "what became of it?"

"If Henry had had it with him, they would have found it," Callie asserted.

"Which probably means Henry didn't have it with him."

Her hand closed over his sleeve. "What could he have done with it? Do you think he might have feared the possibility of a confrontation with Anne's half brother or uncle?"

"He might have." The newspaper slid to the floor, but he paid it no heed. He stared into space, eyes bright in the candlelight, his expression alert. "Yes, if they'd seemed suspicious, Henry certainly would not have come for Anne carrying all that wealth with him, where her family could catch them and demand it back. So he might have hidden the money somewhere before coming to meet Anne, planning for the two of them to retrieve it once they were sure no one followed. Only he was right, and they caught him and killed him, only to discover they'd been a bit hasty."

"That must have been quite a shock to them. They probably," she added with a measure of satisfaction, "thought it a judgment on them. But where would Henry have hidden the money?"

Tony turned his considering regard on her. "You have a devious mind."

"Thank you." She made a pretense of a curtsy from her kneeling position.

"What would you have done with it?" he went on, ignoring her interruption.

"Hidden it somewhere where it wouldn't be found," she said promptly.

"Minx. That's obvious." He smoothed back the hair from her forehead, leaving his hand to rest casually on her shoulder. "He would have feared pursuit from his own family, so he wouldn't have left it at the Gables, and he had reason to fear an ambush here. So he would have left it somewhere in between."

His touch warmed her and set her heart beating faster. Was this how Anne felt when Henry touched her? Breathless, nervous, longing for the contact to continue, yet fearing the unsettled sensations that swept over her? This was all unfamiliar to her; her childhood infatuation for him had never included such tumultuous emotions as these.

"What? No suggestions?" he demanded in mock startlement.

"Idiot," she responded, finding refuge in old patterns. *Beloved idiot,* she corrected mentally. "I was just trying to think what hiding places might exist on the path between the houses."

"Many," he said grimly. "Lord, it's been open parkland for generations. Do you suppose Anne knew of his plan?"

Callie shook her head. It would be better for her concentration if he moved his hand from her. Of course, she could move, but not for anything would she break the contact. "If Anne had known, she would have gone there when he didn't show up for her. And when she found their treasure, she would have known something had gone wrong."

"Perhaps she did just that, then confronted her brother and uncle."

Again, Callie shook her head. "She would have demanded justice for her Henry. We can be fairly sure they didn't kill her as well, and I cannot believe she would have thrown herself from the tower without decrying Henry's murderers. I'm sure she didn't know the truth."

"Which brings us back to where he hid the fortunes." He withdrew his hand then to rub the bridge of his nose. "Do you suppose he did it on the spur of the moment, or do you think he planned it in advance?"

"I don't know." She longed for him to touch her again, yet knew it was foolish of her. With an effort, she kept her thoughts on the matter at hand. "He'd want something he knew to be safe, yet he wouldn't have planned to use it for long." She considered. "Do you know, Henry's letters implied the Lambeths had discouraged the romance." She tilted her head to one side. "Do you think he and Anne had a secret place to pass their letters back and forth?"

"Now, that's an idea." He tapped his finger thoughtfully on the paper, looking at it with unfocused eyes. "Where? Remember, it would have to big enough to hide the money, not just a folded sheet of paper."

"If only—" She broke off, looking up at him with sudden hope. "Maybe they did!"

"Did what?"

"Leave us a clue! No, not on purpose, but unintentionally. Perhaps in the letters they name meeting places."

"You read them. Did they?"

She hesitated, casting her mind back over the impassioned words Henry had penned to his beloved. "N—no," she admitted at last. "Not openly, at least." She brightened. "Perhaps he alluded to their next rendezvous in veiled terms, in case her family got hold of the missive."

"It's a possibility." He held out his hand. "Let's have a look."

Eager now, she hurried to the table where

she had set down the neatly tied bundle. They should start with the final one, then work their way backwards until they found something—anything—that might be a clue. She knelt once more at Tony's side, handed him one, and went to work, concentrating on each word, searching for possible hidden meanings.

"I rather like the notion that the couple should 'bury their past,' " Tony said. "Do you suppose he means they should meet in the family crypt?"

"What wonderful, romantic notions you do have," she retorted, and fought back a yawn.

"It's late," he said abruptly.

She nodded, aware her eyes were so tired she could barely make out the spidery scrawl. If she kept going tonight, she would probably miss the most blatant of hints. "We'd do best to sleep now, and begin again in the morning when we're fresh."

"I'm driving out first thing to inspect the harvest." A touch of regret colored his tone. "You'll have to read the lot, I fear."

She shook her head in pretended dismay. "I knew you weren't really interested." But he was! The light was back in his eyes, the dejection gone from his tired shoulders. He still welcomed a challenge, and she would see to it that he enjoyed this one in full measure.

They mounted the stairs together in tired but companionable silence, and as she crawled between the sheets at last, she found herself all eagerness for the morning to come so she could renew her search. Only this time, it would not be for information about Anne, but for her family's lost fortune—and for the child-hood idol she had begun to glimpse once more.

Eleven

The threatened rain came during the night, soft at first, then whipping into a pounding rage. It awakened Tony, but he could do nothing but go to his window and stare out, willing it to cease, willing the unharvested crops to be spared. But the storm continued, and at last he returned to his bed, knowing he'd need whatever rest he could get. The day ahead threatened to be a difficult one.

As morning approached, the onslaught at last slackened to a gentle patter, then gave way altogether. Tony remained between sheets only until the first pale rays of sunlight filtered into his room. He then returned to his vigil at the window, where dark clouds filling the sky greeted him. On the ground, as far as he could see, the rain had saturated the earth, forming puddles in every depression. Yet as he watched, the clouds blew apart, revealing patches of pale blue like the promise of hope.

He'd risen early; unless the storm had disturbed Callie, even she would not yet be about. Thinking of her made him smile, eased his tension from his troubled night. As his valet helped him to dress, he allowed his thoughts to dwell on her. She was as tenacious as ever, he reflected as he donned his riding coat and eased his injured leg into the top-boots Fimber held. She refused to let go of her adventure, holding onto it with a dream of finding treasure.

Very much, he feared, like a dog worrying a bone that had no meat left on it.

They'd talked a great deal of nonsense the night before. Intriguing, true, but nonsense all the same. A fortune in jewels and coin would hardly have remained hidden for a hundred years without someone stumbling across it. Still, he would not deny her the thrill of her hunt. It would do her no harm, and he could enjoy her enthusiasm.

And what if, by some miracle, she found it? A rush of anticipation surged through him, which he banished, albeit with regret. If she did find it, it would be hers, both by inheritance and by the right of discovery. He'd be glad for her. It would free her to choose her own future, not accept the one thrust upon her.

He adjusted the folds of his neckcloth, approved the image that stared back at him from the cheval glass, and made his way downstairs. She'd fallen into old habits in her dealings with him, he'd noticed; he'd detected the old warmth in her manner, even seen the light of her old hero worship shining in her eyes.

They could share a very companionable marriage.

His steps slowed as he neared the breakfast parlor. A companionable marriage. Only a few days ago, that had been his intent, his greatest hope. But was it fair to her? What chance had she ever had to meet modish young gentlemen? Corinthians, Bucks, Dandies, Tulips, what did she know of them? She'd been pitchforked by poverty from her own schoolroom to that of her charges when she became a governess. She'd not enjoyed a Season, not enjoyed the chance to meet a variety of gentlemen. He was all she had ever known. It would be no great wonder if she mistook a childhood fondness for love. She had no experience of the real thing.

To marry her before she had a chance to unfurl her wings, to discover the power of her smile, would be selfish of him and unforgivably unfair to her. He could not so take advantage of her just because he needed her. She deserved so much more.

He had barely seated himself at his breakfast when Bradshaw, his estate agent, made a deferential entrance. The man cleared his throat, but the distress in his face spoke more eloquently than any words. Tony's heart sank. "What's happened?" he asked, resigning himself to more bad news.

"One of the tide cottages, m'lord. The Appletons." Bradshaw wrung his hands. "During the night. One of the walls collapsed."

"My God." Tony rose. "How is the family?"

"Sam Appleton has broken his arm, and his eldest boy—that's Jimmy—he has some fairly severe cuts, but that, thank heaven, is the worst of it. His wife and the two younger children got out with no more than a handful of bruises between them."

"I'll go at once." He started for the door.

Bradshaw didn't move from it. "There's more, m'lord."

Tony braced himself, waiting.

"The barn where we'd stowed the crops—" Bradshaw broke off, then continued with an obvious effort. "It leaked badly."

"The crop?"

"Drenched, m'lord. They're at it already, trying to save what they can, but the fields have been battered. We need everyone out there if we're to keep it from rotting."

Tony's jaw clenched. Most of the first day's harvest lost . . . Normally that wouldn't be a disaster, but now every penny counted. And there'd be the barn to repair, or they'd lose even more. What they'd be able to salvage from the harvest would barely dent the surface of the problems.

If only he'd been able to ride out there himself, if he'd been able to see with his own eyes the state of that barn . . . or the cottage that collapsed . . .

The plight of his tenants mattered the most. He sent for his curricle, but while he waited he found he had no appetite left for his breakfast. Instead, he ordered most of it packed to be carried with him. There'd be at least one very hungry and tired family trying to salvage what they could from the wreckage of their home.

Half an hour later, when he drove up the muddied track and through the rickety farm gate, a ragged, mud-smeared boy of no more than eleven welcomed him to the wreckage of what had once been a well-kept cottage sur-

rounded by a lovingly tended garden. Roses
and lavender now lay covered in tumbled stone,
and chairs and chests stood piled together in
a sorry heap, topped by mattresses and bed-
ding. Mrs. Appleton followed the lad through
the doorway, her skirts and face filthy, her
shoulders drooping. A younger boy and girl
clung to her dirtied apron, hindering her
movements.

A coldness settled in Tony's stomach as he
took in the sight. His rapid questions confirmed Bradshaw's report—the physical injuries
were not of a serious nature, more of an incon-
venience, but the toll on the family's spirits ran
much deeper. Their home, the center and stability of their lives, would need extensive repairs before the family could return to the
shelter of its roof again.

"They can't stay here," he said to Bradshaw,
who occupied the seat in the curricle beside
him.

"No, m'lord, but it won't be easy to find
them another place."

"Have you family?" Tony asked Mrs. Appleton.

"Aye, m'lord, that we 'ave. I've a sister as lives
in Bath with 'er 'usband who works for a chan-
dler, but they 'aven't room for their own brood,
let alone ours. And Appleton's folk were car-
ters, and have moved up to London."

"What do we have?" Tony looked to Bradshaw.

The estate manager shook his head. "There's
not a single cottage left vacant, and though
they might put up in one of the barns—"

"No!" Tony considered a minute. "We're understaffed at the house at the moment. There should be rooms in the servants' wing."

Mrs. Appleton, who had come to stand near the carriage to speak with him, looked dismayed. She bobbed an uncertain curtsy. "Thanking you kindly, m'lord, but your folks may not take to that."

Bradshaw gave a deprecating cough. "I think you'll find yourselves welcomed warmly, ma'am. There's not a person on this estate, either on the farms or in the house, who doesn't know what his lordship is up against. They'll be only too glad to give you a hand. It will let them know they're a part of the effort."

The woman's troubled expression eased. "Well, that's all right then, if that's the way it is. I wouldn't want to go putting anyone out. They needn't worry, we'll do our share of work, and not get in anyone's way."

Tony left them with the packaged breakfast and orders to pack up what they would need. Turning his horses, he headed toward the barn and its ravaged crop. He only wished he could hit upon as satisfactory a temporary solution to its problems.

They had driven for some little time before it occurred to Tony that Bradshaw, who normally kept up a steady, cheerful flow of conversation, had fallen into an unnatural silence. He cast a sideways glance at the man and noted the deep crease in his brow. "All right," he said on a note of forced cheerfulness, "you might as well tell me the rest. What have you been keeping from me?"

"Not keeping from you, precisely." Bradshaw hesitated. "I hadn't meant to bring it up until after the harvest."

"But now that the harvest seems to be in danger?" Tony prodded.

"It's the loans your brother took out," said Bradshaw, taking the plunge. "The quarter day has passed. They will require payments, I'm afraid."

Loan payments. Tony didn't even bother making the mental calculations necessary to give him a revised total of his indebtedness. Somehow, he'd meet this pressing obligation. But there went more of the monies his tenants needed so badly.

Callie, curled on a sofa with Percival on her lap and the rotund Marmaduke on her skirts at her side, watched Tony's return through the window. From the set of his shoulders, she guessed his morning's expedition had not gone well. The rain, she supposed, and wondered how much damage the crops had suffered.

She waited in growing impatience, but he did not put in an appearance. Which must mean he'd retired to the estate room. Evicting the cats from their chosen positions, she went in search of him.

She found him at his desk, the account books open before him, but his gaze fixed pensively on the wall opposite. He seemed oblivious to her presence. She waited a moment, then cleared her throat. "It's an interesting pattern," she said conversationally.

He started and looked toward her. "I beg your pardon?"

"I merely said the wallpaper has an interesting pattern. At least you seem to think so."

He didn't rise to her fly. Instead, he lowered his gaze to the carefully written sheets before him, then looked back up at her. "Did you want me for something?"

"Yes, you promised to help me with our treasure hunt."

"Did I?" He frowned. "I'm sorry, I'm afraid I can't this morning."

"Can't?" She studied his face, observing the deep lines that etched about his mouth, the tiredness that sat heavily on his brow, the dejection that drooped his shoulders. "Don't want to, you mean." She sighed heavily and shook her head in exaggerated dismay. "I always suspected you had no real interest in fortunes gone astray."

He regarded her through half-lidded eyes. "I need to think."

She tilted her head to one side. "Do you know, there are some people who might take that comment as a hint."

"You do not appear to be of their number." He managed something too troubled to pass for a smile. "I'm sorry I can't help you."

"Oh, don't let it be of any concern," she said airily. "I feel certain Felix will be only too delighted to lend me a hand."

"Good," he responded, thus displaying how little attention he paid to her words. Already, his gaze had unfocused once more, a sure sign he was deep into his own thoughts.

Callie watched him for a full minute longer, then slipped out the door. When Tony wouldn't argue with her, or even make a joke about Felix, something serious troubled him indeed. This was not, she wagered, the time to try to rally him from his depression. That didn't mean she would give up trying to help though.

His need for money lay at the root of his abstraction, that she knew well. She could think of only one possible way to assist. Her mind made up, she set off in search of Felix.

That gentleman was nowhere to be found. Frustrated, Callie made her way up the stairs, only to pause as Marianne's voice drifted down the corridor. Callie set off in pursuit, following the sound to the door of the Ladies' Sitting Room, the sunny chamber on the south side of the rambling old house, long established as Lady Agatha's private retreat.

She looked in and saw that lady seated at her writing desk, a bored expression in her weary eyes. Marianne sat in a wingback chair drawn up near the desk, half her attention on setting neat stitches in her embroidery, the rest focused on some *on dit* picked up in London which she related in never-ending detail.

Lady Agatha looked up with relief at Callie's entrance. "There you are," she said with all the satisfaction of one who had been hunting her quarry for hours. "Why do you not take Marianne for a stroll in the shrubbery? It is not good for her to remain indoors all day."

"It is quite wet out, still," Marianne protested. "It would ruin my slippers."

"Then put on half boots," Callie ordered,

correctly identifying Lady Agatha's request as a plea for help. That lady preferred to be on the telling end of any gossip being exchanged. "I count on you to bear me company. I have a particular favor to ask of you. Do come."

Intrigued, Marianne folded away her stitchery, apologized to Lady Agatha for abandoning her, and promised to finish her tale at the earliest opportunity. Callie bore her from the room before Lady Agatha could assure her there would be no need.

"What may I do for you?" Marianne asked as the two ladies made their way to her chamber.

Quickly, Callie filled her in on the results of studying the letter the night before, and her conclusion that the treasure might lie hidden somewhere on the grounds.

Marianne stared at her in awe. "A fortune? Why did you not tell me of this at once! Oh, Miss Rycroft, if it were but true! No, I dare not hope. It is unkind of you to tease me so. Do you really think there is a chance?"

"There must be. Tony found what might be a clue in one of Henry's last letters to Anne—a hint at what might be their next meeting place."

"Let us go there at once!"

"Do you know where Felix is?" Callie asked.

Marianne froze. "I believe he said he would retire to the billiards room this morning. You do not mean to disturb him, do you?"

"I am very much afraid we will need his assistance. Join us there as soon as you are ready." With that, she left the girl to change her footwear into something more practical. Callie did the same, then made her way to the large chamber where she remembered Tony's father and brother spending a great deal of their time. As she approached, the telltale click of the balls reached her.

She entered silently and waited while Felix lined up his next shot and took it. "Well done," she exclaimed as he straightened at last. "I never could make a clean break."

He leaned back against the table, eyeing her with no little suspicion. "You are up to something, Callie. Whatever it is, I refuse utterly to be any part of it."

"Really, Felix." She strolled into the room and picked up another cue. "Lady Lambeth and I are quite counting on you."

"That settles it, then. If Marianne is with you, I most certainly will not be."

"Not even to recover my lost fortune?"

He set down his cue. "I realize you find it impossible to be serious, even for a moment, but—"

"But I am. Very serious. I think I know where Henry may have hidden the money before he was murdered."

"Good God." He stared at her. "Then what do you need me for? Get Tony to help."

"I want to surprise him."

He snorted. "He turned you down, you mean. Can't say I blame him."

"But wouldn't you just love to find it for him?"

That stopped Felix. A reluctant grin tugged at his mouth. "Wouldn't I, though! Lord, just to see his face would be worth joining in one of your harebrained stunts. All right. Where do you think it is?"

"In the crypt."

"The—" His pained expression returned. "Oh, no, m'girl. I should have known this was all just one of your Banbury tales. I'm not swallowing that plumper."

"But it's not! Honestly, Felix, you can be as bad as Tony sometimes. I'm perfectly serious. I'll show you the spot in the letter if you don't believe me."

Marianne stepped into the room and looked from one to the other of them, her expression guarded. "Is there a problem?"

Felix regarded the girl for a moment, then returned his attention to Callie. "You've gotten *her* to agree to this escapade of yours?"

Marianne straightened. "Of course I intend to help my dear Miss Rycroft. And Tony. Only think what it would mean if we could find all that money!"

"I am thinking." Felix frowned at her. "I still cannot believe you've agreed to this."

"Then you must have a shockingly low opinion of me." Chin tilted high, she left the room. "Where do we go, Miss Rycroft?" she asked over her shoulder.

"Hah! So you haven't told her! I knew it!"

"Oh, do be quiet, Felix. We are going to the family crypt," she added to Marianne.

The girl stopped. "The—" She shook her head. "You cannot mean it!"

"What, afraid of ghosts?" Felix asked. "And

here I thought you and Anne were getting along famously."

Marianne shivered. "N—no. I don't think there will be any ghosts out there. It is just— Oh, explaining anything to you about sensibilities is useless."

"You are welcome to stay behind if you wish," he suggested. "Are you coming, Callie?"

He'd agreed. Relieved to have his muscle, Callie hurried after him, leaving Marianne to follow. As they strode across the drenched lawn toward the small stand of cypress trees which a long-forgotten Lambeth had planted around the ancient mausoleum, Callie experienced a measure of unease. Not for worlds would she admit to this, for Felix would roast her unmercifully, and Marianne, who huddled beside her in obvious distress, needed only the slightest encouragement to flee.

It had never frightened her before, Callie reminded herself. The moss-covered stone structure lay just off the path that led from the Grange to her old home at The Gables; they had played games there, sheltered from sudden showers. And now it might hold a brighter future for them all.

Rust encrusted the iron gate, which stretched across the opening. Callie circled to the left, felt along the niches in the rough carving, and found the age-old key. "I was half-afraid it might have gone," she said, as she slid it into the lock.

"Don't you mean afraid it would still be here?" Marianne shivered, then gave a startled scream as the corroded lock creaked eerily open.

The gate wouldn't budge. Felix grasped one side and hauled, until it at last yielded with a screeching protest that could well have awakened the occupants within. Fighting off that unwelcome reflection, Callie slipped inside, and the cloying tendrils of a spiderweb wrapped about her face. She came within a hair's breadth of imitating one of Marianne's shrieks; but she was made of sterner stuff than that, she informed herself as she swallowed the cry. She would not turn tail and run. She would do what she had come to do, for Tony's sake.

"Felix?" She had to struggle to keep her voice calm. "Would you hand me a branch? The spiders seem to have gotten here first."

Marianne moaned. Felix searched out a long stick and presented it to Callie with due ceremony. He then armed himself with another, and joined Callie as she eyed the web-infested tomb in uncertainty.

Twelve crypts, four on each of the three sides, faced the interior. All sealed. She studied each one in turn, seeking any crevice, niche, or urn that might have served Henry for a hiding place for his cache. Nothing obvious sprang to her attention.

Felix glanced over his shoulder at Marianne. "Aren't you coming in?"

"How can you be so casual about it?" Her voice wavered, as if she were on the verge of tears. "Miss Rycroft, I do wish you would not stay in there. Surely you can see all there is to see from out here."

"That is precisely what I cannot do. If it is here, Henry hid it well." Callie inched forward a step, battling aside the clinging tendrils as she continued her fruitless survey.

"If you are truly afraid, you should go back to the house," Felix suggested, sounding almost sympathetic.

"I—I couldn't," breathed Marianne. "It is so very far. I would rather stay with you—both." Only the slightest pause sounded between the two words.

"Don't be foolish," Felix moved outside to where Marianne shivered, her arms folded about herself. "Come, I'll take you back."

"And leave Miss Rycroft? Oh, no, we couldn't! It would be too dreadful of us. I'll wait."

"Brave of you," Felix said.

She shook her head, refusing to look up at him. "I am not brave at all—as you know perfectly well. Only I could never desert her in there. It's only—" She broke off, trembling.

"There, now, there's nothing to harm you." Felix took a step closer and slid an arm about her shoulders, drawing her near. Marianne stiffened, then, with a soft sob, turned her face against his shoulder. As if of its own volition, Felix's other arm encircled her. For a long moment he held her close, his cheek pressed against the top of her curls, then an oath escaped him. He freed one hand and tilted the girl's chin up so she looked into his face. A stifled groan sounded in his throat, and he kissed her.

Callie, fully aware of their dilemma, looked

away to allow them what privacy she could. Only one practical course of action to help them—and Tony—sprang to her mind. Grabbing a firm hold on her courage, she advanced farther into the tomb and began an inch-by-inch examination of the stone and marble surfaces.

"Felix," Marianne's whisper carried across the dank space. "Oh, Felix."

"Hush, my love. I shouldn't have, but there is only so much a man can take. Hush, do not cry, dearest."

"I—I never dared hope—" Marianne broke off.

"There is nothing to hope for." His voice sounded harsh. "I have loved you from the first moment I set eyes on you, at that damned party where they betrothed you to Reginald. I could say nothing then, and the circumstances haven't changed in the least. I am still not in a position to speak."

A shaky laugh escaped her. "You just spoke quite eloquently, and without voicing a single word."

"I did, didn't I?" A touch of the customary smugness crept back into his voice. "Perhaps we should discuss it again."

Silence fell behind Callie. She reached the end of one wall, waved her stick to clear dirt-shrouded filaments from the next section, and caught back a scream as a giant spider scurried along the remnants of its web to safety. Her flesh crawled with the conviction that thousands of the little creatures clambered over the toes of her half boots and ventured up her stockings. She did this for Tony, she reminded herself as she cast an uneasy glance over her shoulder. Partially reassured that armies of eight-legged terrors did not, in fact, stalk her, she returned to her search.

Yet despite the care with which she examined the dust-encrusted surfaces, she found nothing. If Henry had indeed entrusted his treasure to the safekeeping of the Lambeth ancestors, he had to have stowed it within some secret place of concealment. But how likely would that be? A priest's hole in the house had served a practical function when it had been built. But what purpose would a secret hiding place serve in a mausoleum? The idea was absurd. A broken corner—of which there were none—or a decorative urn—of which there were also none—could have been put to an impromptu use. The idea of secret panels or trap doors was ridiculous. She searched for one anyway.

"I am a cad," Felix declared in heartfelt accents from behind her. "I have fought so hard to prevent this moment from happening, then I ruin all by succumbing to temptation."

Callie turned from her probing to regard them. There came a time, she felt, when purity of motive became a wasted effort. "There is nothing for it but for you to marry her."

Felix looked up. "Do you think I haven't sought some means to bring that about? How could I support her?"

Callie sat back on her heels. "Can you truly think of no occupation to which you might set your hand?"

"How can you ask it of him?" Marianne demanded. "He was born to hold a deck of cards or a dice cup. Have you not seen him at play?"

"On the contrary," Callie said dryly. "Many times. He holds my vowels to prove it."

"And would they were for real, rather than imaginary, sums," sighed Felix. "I was not bred for any occupation other than the gaming tables."

Callie rose from where she had been examining the bottom corner. "You could not possibly win a fortune?"

He shook his head. "It is far easier to lose one, m'girl. How can I ask her to defy her mama and brother to marry a worthless gamester?"

"You are not worthless!" Marianne protested.

"Well, we shall just have to find Henry's fortune." Callie cast a jaundiced eye over the remaining stretch of smooth stone. Not a single hiding place. For that matter, she had seen no sign of Anne's ghostly presence. It occurred to her, depressingly, that she had just faced a crypt full of spiders for nothing.

Felix watched her somberly. "We don't even know for certain if this fortune has any existence outside of your vivid imagination."

"We know Henry was murdered for it," Callie asserted.

"And it is possible Quentin and Cedric did get their hands on it—or possibly only one did, and lied about it to the other. Whoever had it would have found a way to use it stealthily, so no one would question a sudden influx of wealth."

Callie closed her eyes. Could that be true?

"No," she declared with more conviction than she really felt. "Tony needs the money. We will find it." She turned on her heel, strode outside, and shoved at the iron grating.

Felix took it from her and forced it closed once more. With a hand that shook, Callie relocked it, returned the key to its hiding place, and stalked back toward the house.

"Where are you going?" Felix demanded as he and Marianne caught up to her.

"To reread those letters! There must be a clue in there somewhere, and I won't give up until I've found it."

Felix gave an exaggerated sigh. "I think," he informed Marianne, "we have a very long day ahead of us."

Twelve

Callie handed the last letter to Marianne, who sat at her side in the Blue Salon, and glared across at the gilt-edged mirror which now reflected only the everyday view of the room.

"Nothing?" asked Felix. He sounded weary, as were they all from their fruitless task.

"Nothing," Callie confirmed. "Unless either of you could find something I missed."

Marianne sighed. "Perhaps there is no more meaning in these than the obvious. 'Bury our past among the dead and build a new life,'" she read from the sheet she held. "If only that were possible."

Felix rose and came to stand behind her, his hands resting gently on her shoulders. "It must be possible," he declared.

"But how?" cried Marianne. "No, we have been over it already. I can see no way unless we abscond with a fortune the way Anne and Henry planned."

"Only they weren't taking it for themselves, but for the Stuart cause," Callie reminded her.

"And we haven't a fortune with which to abscond," added Felix. "Building a new life requires every bit as much money as building a new house."

"Building—" Callie broke off and stared at him. "Felix, I never thought I should have reason to say it, but you are a genius!"

"I had been wondering when you would realize it," he responded promptly, but with considerable suspicion. "What, may I ask, has prompted your startling revelation?"

"Building!" she repeated. "We investigated the burying of the past, but what about the building of the new future?"

He considered, while Marianne looked up at him over her shoulder with adoration and hope in her eyes. An arrested expression settled over his aquiline features. *"Building?* Do you think—"

"Yes! Even if he never meant his words as a clue, this makes perfect sense! What better place to hide something than where everything is in chaos? What we need to find," she added as she sprang to her feet, "is a place where something new was being built, or something old being repaired. Don't you see?" she added at her audience's blank incomprehension. "He would only have meant to leave the jewels for a little while, perhaps an hour at most. A pile of bricks or stone would have made a perfect hiding place."

Felix shook his head sadly. "No. I never would have taken you for such a bubble-headed female, Callie. Only consider. His treasure would have stayed out of sight only until the building continued the next day. As soon as the supplies were moved, it would have been un-covered."

"Then he must have been more careful in his hiding." She paced the length of the room, trying to hit upon anything that might give her the inspiration she needed. "What if he thought he were being followed?" she asked the other two. "He might have concealed it somewhere where they simply built over it with-out ever realizing what lay beneath."

Felix opened his mouth, but the skepticism in his face faded to speculation. "That's possi-ble," he said at last. "It certainly makes more sense than that little expedition of yours to the crypt."

She waved that aside. "We have to find out what—"

"If anything," stuck in Felix.

"—was being built at the time Anne died," Callie finished, ignoring Felix.

"I fear another trip to the muniments room," he told Marianne as Callie started to-ward the door.

But that was not Callie's first destination. She threaded her way through the corridors until she reached the estate office. There she found Tony, slumped at the great desk, his gaze un-focused as he stared unseeingly at one of Brad-shaw's extensive lists. Harold, sprawled on the floor near his master's feet, thumped a perfunc-tory tail in greeting.

Tony looked up, and his heavy frown eased. "Whatever have you been about?" he de-manded. "You look like a ragamuffin!"

She glanced in a little surprise at her dress,

which bore liberal smears of dirt, dust, and mildew. "Oh. The mausoleum. Really, Tony, your mama simply must have a talk with the maids. First the attics and now the crypt."

More lines of tension faded from his brow. "And having spent an inspiring morning among my ancestors, what are you about, now?"

"Construction." Briefly, she explained her latest conclusions.

He regarded her in a mixture of amusement and consternation. "And you now intend to dismantle my home, stone by stone? What delightful ideas you have."

"Not the *whole* house, idiot. Only any portions that might have been under repair at the right time."

"And just what do you intend to do if you learn that—oh, for example, the kitchens were remodeled? You can't go about tearing down walls."

"Why can't I? Oh, I don't mean anything extensive or damaging, but—"

"And just how much do you consider 'extensive or damaging'?" he demanded.

"Honestly!" She glared at him. "One would think you had no interest at all in finding this fortune."

"One might think I had some small interest in preserving my home from a Bedlamite who intended to dismantle it!"

Her sudden temper evaporated as she realized she'd jarred him out of his depression. "Then you had better accompany me to make sure I don't do any real damage, hadn't you?"

With that, she turned on her heel and marched out the door, slamming it behind her.

In the hall, she began to count. Before she reached five, the handle rattled, he pulled the door open and burst out, only to halt abruptly as he ran into her.

"I beg your pardon," he said stiffly.

Callie, who found herself pressed warmly against him, his right arm about her to steady her, couldn't think of a single thing about which to complain. "In the old days," she said, somewhat breathless, "you would have made it out by the count of three."

"Minx. In the old days I would have—" He broke off and moved away from her. "What did it take me now, until twenty?"

"Oh, you made remarkable speed." She took his arm as casually as she might have done ten years previously, only this time the act was anything but casual. It seemed crazy that something could feel so normal, yet cause such a nervous, dancing sensation in her stomach and make her afraid to look at him. She wasn't afraid of anything.

Or was she? She stole a look at him, and sensed a tension almost equal to her own. Did he regret his offer for her? He was healing; both his injury and his spirits improved. Not much longer and he would be ready to resume the activities customary for a gentleman of fashion. He wouldn't need her anymore.

That, she feared.

Their going their separate ways hadn't troubled her during those several years they had been apart. But it was different now. Why, exactly, she still couldn't be sure. But it was very different.

They entered the muniments room followed by the gray-and-white Percival. Tony stooped to stroke the animal that stropped itself against his top boot. "I suppose you're going to tell me what we're doing in here? Or do you intend to dismantle every single room, and simply decided to begin with this one?"

"The building records." She crossed to the wall housing the collection of estate books, then moved along it until she reached the volume covering the correct years.

"Here, it's heavy." Tony drew it out for her and carried it to the table.

She regarded him through half-lidded eyes. "You think I couldn't carry that?"

"Would you rather argue or look for this treasure trove of yours?" he demanded, and began leafing through the book.

"Can't I do both?" She joined him, peering over his shoulder at the motley collection of fists that inscribed the pages.

He ran a finger along entries rendered in a spidery hand, accounts of crops planted and cottages repaired. The purchase of a new carriage had been carefully recorded, along with the comment that the current carriage house needed a wall shored up, and a grain bin needed a new top. He paused, glancing at Callie. "What do you think?"

Callie reread the passage, hope growing. "Was the work done?" she demanded.

"We'll find out." He continued his careful examination of each line until, four pages later, he pointed out the disbursement of sufficient funds to pay for the necessary materials.

Callie studied it, frowning. "They didn't buy much."

"Just an added support," Tony reminded her. "I think I even know where it is."

She closed her eyes, envisioning the low stone building bordering the cobbled yard with the stalls opening off it. "That buttress we used to hide behind when we played games?" she hazarded. A sudden, vivid memory assailed her, of crouching low, pressed close to Tony's side, while Oliver hunted them with a bucket of water from the stables, intent on soaking his quarries before they could reach their home base and safety. He'd found them, and Tony had covered her with his body, shielding her from the drenching as they'd all laughed. All harmless, meaningless fun, but the remembrance sent warmth seeping through her, and filled her with the desire to feel his arms wrapped about her once more.

"Want to have a look at it?" A pale reflection of the old mischievous light glowed in his eyes.

She wouldn't mind hiding there with him again. But that, she felt certain, was not part of his plan.

They started toward the library with its exit leading toward the stables, only to encounter Durstan emerging from that apartment, a harassed expression on his normally impassive countenance. The look faded at sight of them, and he straightened his coat and strode forward, once more the image of the proper butler. "My lord, Mrs. Leeds has arrived."

"Good God." Tony's brow snapped down.

"As you say, m'lord." Durstan stared at a spot just beyond his employer's left shoulder. "Her ladyship is with her in the Gold Salon. I have sent James to locate Lady Lambeth."

"I left her in the Blue Salon," Callie offered.

"Thank you, miss." Durstan permitted himself a paternal smile for her.

"I suppose I had better see what she wants," Tony said as the old retainer retreated toward the nether regions of the house, undoubtedly to see about the ordering of refreshments.

"Who is she?" Callie asked as she fell into step beside him.

"Marianne's mama."

"This should be interesting," came her prompt reply. "I have never seen a dragon in real life."

"What about your erstwhile employer?" he asked.

Callie directed a pained look at him. "The less said about her, the better I shall like it. Though now that I think about it, I doubt it would take much to bully Marianne."

They crossed the Great Hall and entered the elegant sitting room, where Lady Agatha sat enthroned in a wingback chair, her bearing regal as she listened with a wooden expression to her visitor. Before her sat a frail, wilting creature, draped in lavender crepe. Ringlets of silvery white hair escaped from beneath a drooping bonnet boasting a filmy veil, and a pair of watery gray eyes looked out from a face almost devoid of color. A wisp of lace-edged muslin dangled from her thin hand. When she spoke, even her voice would have drooped, if it weren't for the hint of steel underlying the soft, tremulous words.

"And here are Lambeth and Miss Rycroft," Lady Agatha declared, ruthlessly cutting into her guest's monologue at the earliest moment.

Tony advanced to bow over her hand. "An unexpected pleasure, ma'am."

"Lambeth," she murmured in acknowledgement. "And this is Miss Rycroft?" The drooping figure swayed a trifle, turning to bring Callie into her line of vision.

Callie stepped forward as Lady Agatha made the introduction, and found herself scrutinized through a lorgnette with lavender ribands swirling about the handle.

After a long moment, Mrs. Leeds laid it back against her slight bosom. She turned back to Lady Agatha, and with infinite sadness said: "My daughter writes to me that this Miss Rycroft is to marry Lambeth."

Lady Agatha's eyes glittered. "You can have no idea how delighted we all are. Even Marianne, for they have become quite the closest of friends."

Mrs. Leeds slumped in her chair. "The dear child. Always so good to me. Never does she fail to behave as a daughter ought to her poor, widowed mama. But always so willing to see only the best in people." The last she uttered into her trailing handkerchief.

The door opened, and Marianne stepped inside. Felix followed, but remained by the door as the girl hurried forward to kiss her mother's cheek. Callie, who had gained the distinct impression she had been dismissed, dropped back to join him.

"How long since Marianne's papa died?" Callie asked in an undervoice as Durstan arrived with a tray laden with cups, saucers, and a teapot. Albert followed, bearing another with plates filled with innumerable delicacies.

Felix caught a choice slice of almond cake as the footman passed, and received a quelling look from the butler. "Upwards of a dozen years," he said after swallowing a bite "Been in perpetual mourning ever since. It's my guess," he added, for once employing the discretion of lowering his voice, "her papa cocked up his toes rather than stay married to that watering pot. Can't say I blame him."

Lady Agatha poured the tea, and handed a cup to Tony. As he delivered this to Mrs. Leeds, he asked: "To what do we owe the pleasure of this visit?"

"Does a widowed mother need a reason to visit her only daughter?" she said on a quavering sigh. "I have been so lonely since she came here to live. Just to see her is surely reason enough."

"But we only parted a very few days ago," Marianne protested.

Mrs. Leeds waved that aside. "A week in London. So much noise, so much bustle. We scarcely had a chance to be together."

"But you insisted we go shopping every moment," Marianne reminded her.

"Yes, for your sake, my love, for you know that on the pittance I have been allowed as a jointure I cannot purchase such gowns as would become me. And now, to look at you, I see that it has all been worth the sacrifice."

Marianne glanced at her morning gown of peach muslin. "It is quite pretty, of course, but shockingly dear."

"Never have I begrudged a penny of what we have spent for your clothing," her mama assured her.

"Tony is paying for these," Marianne stuck in with uncharacteristic candor.

"And now he shall have the satisfaction of seeing how well such an investment has paid off. My love, I bring you tidings that are certain to bring you delight, for I know how you have hated the distressing state of widowhood."

Marianne flinched. "Indeed, Mama, Lady Agatha and Tony could not have been kinder. They have shown me every consideration—"

"I am sure they have, my love, but no one knows better than I how distressing is the loss of one's life companion, how pitiful is the lot of a mere widow when one has known the joys of being a wife. And not even a home of your own to manage. But now all that will change. My love, I vow I could not be happier for you."

Marianne regarded her steadily. "How will it change, Mama?"

"I have received an offer for your hand," she declared in the tones of one delivering the best of all possible news.

Marianne blanched. She opened her mouth, but no sound came out.

Her mama beamed at her. "Ah, I see you are speechless with delight. How could it be otherwise? I vow, I was so overcome with joy, I was obliged to lie upon my sofa for the remainder of the day, while my dear Purvey waved burnt feathers before me. Such an agreeable shock, but a shock nevertheless, yet one I was only too grateful to endure for your sake. Such a comfort to me, to know you will be so well established, for I know you will not neglect your poor dear mama."

Felix had stiffened at the opening of this speech, and Callie caught his arm, warning him to keep his tongue between his teeth with a shake of her head. He glared at her but kept his peace.

Tony broke the sudden silence. "And may we know the identity of this gentleman?"

Mrs. Leeds dabbed at her eyes. "The earl of Schofield."

"Schofield!" Tony glanced at Marianne, then returned his attention to her mama. "Surely you cannot be serious, madam."

"So very flattering, so very condescending of him, I know. It is so hard to believe her good fortune. You will be a countess, my love. And he is quite rich, and will keep you in the first style of elegance, and we—you will never want for anything."

Marianne, her complexion unnaturally pale, regarded her parent in dismay. "But—he is more than sixty!"

"You must not refine too much upon that, my love. It is true he has not enjoyed the most robust health of late years, but with the proper care, and a loving wife to tend to his every whim, I make certain he will enjoy a great many more years."

Marianne's hands clenched in her lap. "You say he offered for me, Mama?"

"I received his letter by post only yesterday. I vow, I could hardly believe my eyes, and my constitution has never been strong, and my poor Purvey feared it would bring on my palpitations, which she tried to prevent by every means. She was quite distressed at the prospect of my traveling so many miles to see you this day, but I know my duty as your mama, and nothing would keep me from bringing such joyful news to you the moment I recovered enough strength for the journey."

"No." Marianne uttered the word in a flat tone.

Mrs. Leeds patted her hand. "You are quite overcome by your good fortune, and it is no wonder. Such a rise in the world as it will be for you, for Schofield Park must be twice the size of this house, and as for the gardens! They are mentioned in glowing terms in every guide to the noble houses in the land. Indeed, I could not have done better for you had I enjoyed excellent health, which I am sad to say I have never done in my life."

"I said no, Mama." Marianne's voice sounded hollow, but her tone was firm.

Her mama blinked, and her voice took on a sharpened edge. "Whatever can you mean, child?"

Marianne cast a rapid glance at Felix, then turned back to her parent. "I mean I will not marry him."

A soft "Brava" escaped Felix.

"Will not—" Mrs. Leeds forced a shaky

laugh. "This is the merest irritation of the nerves, my love. Quite unbecoming in a lady in your situation. Now, he is quite eager to set a date, and—"

"No. I won't. Listen, Mama," she went on as that lady stared at her in astonishment. "I know that he is very rich, and I would have more pin money than you ever had for your entire house-keeping allowance, but truly, I cannot marry him. I endured one loveless marriage. I am sorry, Lady Agatha," she added to her mother-in-law, "but you know that is true."

Lady Agatha, who had been regarding the girl in fascination, nodded. "Indeed, my dear, anyone who has endured the dubious honor of having been Reginald's wife deserves some measure of happiness in her future."

"Exactly so!" Mrs. Leeds exclaimed. "And how better to achieve this than with an aging husband who will shower every luxury upon her?"

"With a man who loves me!"

"Love!" Mrs. Leeds spoke the word with scorn. "Love does not cover the tradesmen's bills."

"I know that," Marianne said in a choked voice. "But it doesn't matter anymore. I would rather be a pauper for the rest of my life than endure the misery of a loveless marriage again!"

"The life of a pauper," pointed out Mrs. Leeds, "is invariably short as well as unpleasant, my girl." She gave an artistic sniff and buried her face in her lavender-scented handkerchief. "To think my only child would rather abandon me in my widowhood, leave me to suffer the ills of poverty, than to do this one little thing. I had not thought you to be so heartless."

Marianne dropped to her knees before her mother's chair and took the one hand the woman would spare from her handkerchief. "Indeed, I am not your only child. You are forgetting Clyde."

"And well I should, for all he remembers me," her mother snapped. "I could starve in a ditch for all he cares. No, my love, I must pin my hopes on you."

Distressed, Marianne clung to her mother, ready tears filling her eyes and spilling down her cheeks. "You know I should never desert you."

"Then you will marry Schofield?"

"I cannot. Please believe me, for I will not change my mind. I know your life is hard, and I know mine will be the same, but I would gladly endure any hardship for even a few brief years of happiness. To be with the man I love"—and here her gaze flickered across to Felix—"would make everything worthwhile."

Her mama sank back against the cushion and clutched at her heart. A soft moan escaped her. "Wicked, ungrateful girl. To think I should have lived to see the day. Go then, desert me. Leave me to die in my solitude and misery."

"I trust you won't do that, ma'am." Tony, apparently deciding he had endured sufficient Cheltenham tragedy for one day, rose. "Mama, if you will ring for Mrs. Leeds's maid? I feel certain she will be more comfortable in her chamber. And we will have Mrs. Durstan prepare one

of her special draughts." Already, Lady Agatha
pulled the bell rope. "Now, Mrs. Leeds, if you
will permit Marianne to assist you—"

"No!" The voice sounded amazingly strong
for one suffering a spasm. "Wicked girl! She
has cast me off utterly, and I shall have nothing
more to do with her. Get her out of my sight.
If she will not oblige me by doing this one very
small thing—and at such an advantage to herself, to become a countess—then I shall never
set eyes upon her again."

Lady Agatha strode to her side. "Come," she
said in her no-nonsense voice. "You are worn
down from your journey. I will take you to your
room, where you may spend the rest of the day
recovering. And you need not be concerned
with dressing for dinner. I will have a tray sent
up to you." She took the invalid's arm, boosted
her to her feet, and propelled her to the door.

For several seconds after the two women left,
silence reigned in the Gold Salon. Then Felix,
beaming, strode forward, gathered Marianne
into his arms, and swung her off her feet. "Well
done, my love! I must say, you routed the en-
emy in prime style. But it seems you have now
been disowned. Does this mean I may claim
you?"

Marianne burst into tears.

Thirteen

"I still say it was well done of you," announced Felix. He held Marianne close against his side on the sofa in the Blue Salon, to which room Callie had insisted they all remove.

Marianne made use of the handkerchief with which he had generously provided her. "Indeed, it was not. But how could I possibly do as she asked?"

"You could not." He dropped a kiss on her golden curls.

Callie regarded the troubled girl with uncertain solicitude. "Your mama seems to me to be remarkably strong, despite her trailing habits."

"I wish she were, but she is forever suffering a spasm or a fit of the vapors, or going off in strong hysterics." Marianne drooped against Felix's supporting shoulder. "I could never forgive myself if she were to become seriously ill because of me."

"I should be very much surprised if she did." With difficulty, Callie kept the acidity out of her voice. "I imagine when she realizes you are adamant, she will turn to your brother for support."

"But he is forever out of funds," Marianne protested. "All Mama's hopes were pinned on my making an advantageous alliance, and I meant to, truly I did, because I know my duty, except—" she raised her worshipful gaze to Felix's face, "how could I?"

"You couldn't," Felix repeated promptly. "For you to marry a man older than your own papa would be unthinkable. Much better for you to marry me."

Tears brimmed once more in her eyes. "But how are we to contrive that? You know we have thought of everything we could, and still discovered no means."

Felix leaned his chin against her forehead. "I've been thinking about that. Would you mind very much living on the Continent?"

She brightened at once. "Oh, I should like it of all things."

"It would be much less expensive than London," he explained. "Don't fret, love. We'll manage to scrape out a living."

"As long as we are together," Marianne vowed, "nothing else will matter." Her mist-filled eyes sparkled with adoration.

Callie, watching the exchange, experienced a tug of envy. They were wonderful sentiments, all the more so for being shared, but love, without the wherewithal to sustain body and soul, couldn't help but suffer. Worry alone took a dreadful toll on a person. Her gaze strayed to Tony, who had taken no part in the conversation thus far. He gazed moodily into space, but whether his thoughts dwelt on Felix and Marianne's difficulties, or on the progress of the harvest—which seemed most likely—she couldn't tell.

"It's a great pity we won't be able to start our own gaming establishment," Felix continued. "But never mind, love. We'll manage. I know a few people, we'll be able to find a place to stay. What do you say, would you prefer Munich or Rome?"

"Oh, Rome, please," cried Marianne. "I have always dreamed of seeing it."

"And perhaps later," he mused, "when we have ourselves established, we could go to Paris. Ah, I have it!" Enthusiasm lit his entire countenance. "Why do we not start our own establishment in a very small way? We could hold select card parties in our rooms."

"Oh, do you think we could?" Marianne regarded him with delight, her tears of a minute before all but forgotten.

He beamed at her. "Of a certainty. You are the perfect hostess, my love. What more could we need?"

"Money," Callie said bluntly. "No, I don't doubt your ability in the least, Felix. Remember, I have had the dubious pleasure of playing at cards with you. But a little bit of money to fall back on in case of hard times never comes amiss."

"It would be a help," Felix admitted, "but not a necessity."

Marianne slumped. "But where could we get it?"

"There's always Callie's treasure," he reminded her.

"My—" Callie broke off and turned to Tony.

"The treasure!" she exclaimed. "Tony, we forgot about it when Mrs. Leeds arrived."

Felix winced. "What, another visit to the crypt?"

"The carriage house," corrected Tony, dragging himself from his abstraction. At Felix's skeptical look, he explained about the renovations, and the possibility of what might have happened.

Marianne clasped her hands, her whole being radiating hope. "Oh, I do pray you may be right," she breathed. "Only think if we could find it, what it would mean to us all."

Felix looked thoughtful for a minute, then shook his head. "It seems a pretty slim hope to me. That's stone work out there, you know. I don't see how anything could be covered up without the workmen noticing."

"Oh." Marianne's volatile spirits sagged once more. "You don't think a workman found it and—and kept it, do you? Fate could not be so cruel!"

Callie stared at her, appalled, until common sense regained control. "It's not likely," she said with a touch more certainty than she felt. "The grooms would have been about, and other workmen. I don't see how it could have been discovered and kept a secret."

Marianne sighed in relief. "Then we have only to go out there and find it!"

"Assuming it is even there," Tony reminded her. "This is only a guess, and the more I think about it, the less likely it seems."

Callie bristled. "Have you a better suggestion?"

He shook his head. "I wish I did, but I don't."

"And are you willing to give up without a struggle?" she pursued.

"You'd never let me." He evicted Archimedes, who had taken possession of his lap, removed a few black and white cat hairs, and rose. "We might as well get on with it, then."

A preliminary inspection of the carriage house did not prove promising. Not that they had any difficulty in determining the site of that long-ago construction; only one buttress fortified the walls, and its stones showed a faint beige hue instead of the steely gray of the rest of the building. But one look confirmed that it would not be easy for anyone to conceal a small fortune in jewelry and coin within it, without it having been found as soon as the construction work resumed.

Callie stood back, eyeing it with disfavor. "If it had been built in steps," she said at last, "there might have been a chance of something being concealed and staying hidden."

Felix regarded it through his quizzing glass. "It doesn't seem very likely," he agreed. "But to be certain, we would have to destroy it. I cannot speak for you, of course, but at the moment I think I would prefer to investigate other possibilities. Have we any?"

Tony ran his hand along the uneven masonry. "I didn't check all the records," he admitted. "I'm sorry, Callie. This simply isn't wide enough for a space to have been left between the stones. I can have it dismantled, if you like, though."

She laid her hands on the sun-warmed stone, her fingers tracing the lines of mortar and the marks of the chisel. Warm. Shouldn't she be feeling that otherworldly chill if she had found something of importance? She looked around, searching for any sign of the illusive flame. "Anne's not here."

"This may not be her territory," Felix suggested.

"Or she may not be interested in a treasure," added Tony.

"Or we may be in the wrong spot," Callie finished.

Tony shifted his weight—to ease the strain off his injured knee, Callie guessed. This wasn't good for him. It would be best if she could find something for him to do that would keep him off his feet for the rest of the day. Fortunately, just such an occupation lay ready at hand, if she could talk him into it.

"Either we search every inch of these grounds—" she began.

"Which Quentin and Cedric undoubtedly already did," stuck in Felix.

"Or we search the records to see if they carried out any other work at the time," she finished.

"It would be easier than poking into every hollow tree or stump or rabbit hole on the grounds," admitted Marianne, though she sounded doubtful.

They trooped back to the house in a silence born of discouragement. Tony made no demur when Callie escorted him to the muniments room; he merely took his former seat and resumed reading where he had left off. Marmaduke and Harold followed them into the apartment; the spaniel padded in small circles, then flopped down at Tony's feet with a heartfelt sigh. Marmaduke sprawled on an aged carpet in a patch of sun, his sleepy gaze focused on a dust mote that swirled in the light. The oddest sensation crept over Callie that they kept vigil with Tony. She shrugged it off, but still her gaze rested on him for a minute more before she made her thoughtful way to the Blue Salon.

For a very long while, she stood before the mirror, but no ghostly image flickered in its reflective depths. Had Anne, having accomplished her purpose of bringing Henry's murder to light, now lost interest in the people who currently inhabited her home? Without a little more otherworldly help, they might never uncover the treasure—if, indeed, it were still around to be found.

Restless, she prowled the house. She discovered Lady Agatha once more in the Ladies' Sitting Room, writing a lengthy discourse to one of her many acquaintances. Callie left her to it and headed for the library where she could let herself out onto the terrace and indulge her unsettled spirit with a long tramp through the grounds.

As she entered, Felix and Marianne, who had been standing before the hearth entwined in one another's arms, sprang apart. Vexed with herself for disturbing them, Callie started to draw back, then decided this would only embarrass them further. "I'm just going for a walk," she called, and hurried across the room.

She drew back the drapes and ducked out the French windows. The warm sunlight hit her full in the face, and for a moment she considered going back for her bonnet. But not for anything would she interrupt those two again. With a sigh, she set forth down the path that led around the side of the house.

Before her, the long hedge stretched in both directions, marking the gravel walkway. The turn to the left would take her to the lake and the gazebo; the righthand path led to the maze.

She stopped, her mind suddenly racing. She and Tony had glimpsed a ghostly flame along this path, and it had led them to the maze. Did Cedric haunt the gardens, his soul fettered by his murderous crime? A vision sprang to her mind, of Cedric assaulting Henry, striking the fatal blow, then concealing the body within the maze until he could obtain help in disposing of it. She shivered in the warm sunlight. It seemed all too possible. Perhaps that was why Anne seemed to confine herself indoors, to avoid encountering her uncle's guilt-laden spirit.

Of course, there was another possibility. The specter might be Henry, searching in vain for his beloved Anne, knowing even beyond the grave that he had an appointment to meet her that he could not fail to keep. That scenario appealed to her streak of romanticism, but not to her better developed sense of logic. If Henry sought Anne, he would poke about the house.

Besides, she'd sensed guilt and sorrow from this specter. That sounded more like Cedric.

The flicker of something off to her left caught her attention, dragging her from her reverie. She looked, then froze. There, near the hedge, not twenty feet from her, the ghostly flame flickered again. Even as she stared, it shifted and moved away, along the path that led to the lake and the folly beyond.

Callie broke into a run, following as best she could with her hampering narrow skirts. The flame wavered erratically, drifting from side to side, vanishing into the bushes only to appear again the next moment. And always, it led her toward the lake. Then, as abruptly as it had appeared, it flared and extinguished, leaving Callie alone beside the hedge.

Anne. This time, it had been Anne, not the ghost they had seen here before. And Anne wanted her to go this way, toward the lake, not into the maze.

Why had their other specter led them in the other direction? To draw their attention away from the lake—or the folly? Her mind reeling with speculation, she turned on her heel and strode back toward the house.

As she mounted the steps to the terrace, the drapes swung back and Tony emerged. The enthusiasm of his step was marred by the stiffness of his movements; it vexed her that he had not remained still longer. Marianne and Felix crowded behind him, and he came forward, limping but eager.

"They were doing more building," he called as she neared.

"The folly?" she asked.

He halted. "How did you—" He broke off, then hazarded: "Anne?"

She told him of the encounter, including her conclusion that the other specter had been trying to lead them away from their goal. "But it will be the most dreadful mess, if we must tear down the entire structure," she concluded.

"Not to mention bringing my mother's wrath down upon your head." His tired eyes gleamed. "But it shouldn't come to that. It seems that Quentin decided to have the folly floor inlaid with the family coat of arms."

"He did that? Let's see—" She broke off, doing some rapid calculations. "That can be no more than ten feet in diameter. It shouldn't be hard to take up that area."

Tony's sudden grin flashed. "Without inflicting too much damage," he agreed.

Callie turned to stare across the lake. "A hole already cut in the floor would be the perfect hiding place. It is raised about four feet to keep it from the damp, is it not? Then it would have been easy for the workmen to finish their job and never realize something had been inserted underneath."

"Good gad," Felix breathed. "Almost, Callie, you begin to convince me that this is not a complete wild-goose chase."

"Of course it isn't!" Her hands clenched. "It cannot be."

"I admit, I would be very glad if it weren't," Tony declared with more than a touch of his old energy.

Felix drew out his snuffbox and opened it

with an expert flick of his thumb. "And how, might I ask, are we to tear up this work of art? Your laborers, I believe, are busy with the harvest."

Tony straightened. "I'll do it, of course. Or do you wish to announce to the neighborhood that we've gone mad for the hope of a hundred-year-old treasure?"

Felix looked taken aback. "No! I should think not! But do you mean to imply that you intend to go out there with a hammer and whatever other tools would be required and do it yourself?"

"Of course he can't," Callie declared. "You and I will do it, Felix."

"*Me?*" He stared at her as if she had lost her mind. "My dear Callie—"

"Of course, if you have no interest in any of the money, that's up to you," she added sweetly.

"If there even is any." He glared at her.

"And you will do no such thing," Tony informed her. "I said I would do it, and that's exactly what I meant. With Felix's help, of course," he added with a wicked air of innocence.

Callie opened her mouth to protest, but bit it back. Why hadn't she had the sense to keep quiet before? She'd implied Tony wasn't capable of doing heavy work, and now he'd have to prove her wrong. *Men,* she thought in exasperation, and followed the others back inside to change into their oldest clothes.

When she returned downstairs, none of the others waited in the hall. Having no desire to waste time, she headed for the stable to investigate the available tools. She found Tony there before her, garbed in a coat and buckskins that only by some miracle had been spared from a rubbish heap. He looked up at her approach, and a smile of pure enjoyment spread across his strained face.

It stopped Callie like a blow from a bouquet of roses, heady and intoxicating. There he was at last, her childhood idol, restored in spirit if not yet in body. Tall, rugged, handsome—and so much more. The deviltry danced once again in his eyes, the old energy suffused him, reaching out to wrap about her as well, to draw her into his web of laughter and enthusiasm.

She loved him. The certainty washed over her like a tidal wave. She loved him, utterly and completely. Too stunned to move, she simply gazed at him as her mind raced. What would happen, now that he was restored? Would he see in her a romantic princess in desperate need of a knight-errant to rescue her? Or would she remain in his eyes a little girl, capable and temper-driven, that he would tease and dismiss? She held her breath, afraid to break the spell that enveloped her, afraid to initiate the interchange that might all too easily lead to her disenchantment.

His smile faded to a puzzled frown. She found herself incapable of action; she just stood there, staring at him as if she were witless. He shifted his weight, and she swayed toward him, frightened and trembling, her heart beating so hard she felt dizzy. She had certainly never felt any sensations like these around him before. They disoriented her, making her want she knew not what.

The sound of approaching footsteps interrupted her raging thoughts. Marianne, gowned once more in the severest of mourning black, looked into the stable, accompanied by Felix. He had discarded his elaborate wardrobe in favor of an ancient riding coat and a pair of stained buckskins. A hazy comment formed in her mind about the startling alteration to his appearance, but for once she let it pass unspoken.

Felix shook his head sadly. "I thought this was where we'd find you. Do you know, it is positively indecent to be so eager to engage in manual labor."

"Don't you mean in any labor?" Tony turned from Callie to pick up the tools, once more intent on their treasure hunt. He handed a saw and crowbar to Felix, and himself took a hammer and shovel. Together, they set forth to the far side of the lake.

What would have happened, Callie wondered as she hurried after them, if the other two hadn't come bursting onto the scene? Probably nothing, her innate honesty warned her. She had certainly reacted to his presence, but had he done the same to hers? She had no idea, and she desperately needed to know.

Despite what she suspected to be his best efforts to disguise his limp, she could tell that his knee pained him considerably. Still, the enjoyment remained in his eyes, and his smile, when he caught her glance, warmed her with the sense that it was special, meant for her alone.

"Where did you see Anne?" he asked as they crossed the scythed lawn toward the gravel path.

"Just up there." She gestured. "She's not there now," she added.

"Never mind. Maybe she'll be waiting for us in the folly."

She was. Callie felt the spectral presence as soon as she stepped through the doorway. She shivered, and scanned the dimness for any sign of a flickering flame.

Marianne, just behind her, stopped beneath the arched opening. "Are you certain we ought to do this?" she asked, her voice quavering.

"Yes." Callie stepped aside, moving to where she could study the family coat of arms that workmen had skillfully inlaid into the wood. "It does seem a shame to take up their work," she said.

Tony set down his tools and joined her. "I cannot say I share Quentin's taste."

"Does that mean we can just tear this out?" Felix regarded the marquetry with disapprobation. "It would save a great deal of trouble if we didn't have to be careful. I always thought it a particularly revolting floor decoration, anyway."

"If you do so," came Lady Agatha's voice from behind him, "you will never sit down to one of Armand's meals again."

Tony looked up. "I wondered if you would join us."

"Someone must make certain that you do not destroy our heritage." She seated herself on one of the chairs along the wall. Marianne took the one at her side, leaving Callie, Felix, and Tony to eye the inlay work with disfavor.

"Right here?" Tony asked, pointing with the shovel to a spot directly in front of him.

Felix sighed, dragged off his coat, and knelt on the floorboards. Tony followed suit; Callie winced at the pain that flashed across his face, though he made no sound of protest.

"Callie," he said, his voice sounding tight. "Will you hand me the hammer?" And with that, they set to work pulling nails.

Callie dropped to her knees beside them, her excitement growing with each nail that pulled free with a protesting shriek. The flicker toward the middle of the design caught her attention, and she touched Tony's sleeve. "She's here," she breathed, then looked up to see Lady Agatha and Marianne staring at the spectral apparition in fascinated horror.

"I begin to believe you may be right, Calpurnia," said Lady Agatha.

With the aid of the crowbar, Tony removed the first of the planks. Felix took it from him, then set to work with the saw. The minutes crept by, and the hole before them grew until one of them could scramble through it.

Felix, with a satisfied grunt, pulled on one more board, but it refused to come free. "It's stuck," he protested, and peered through the hole into the darkness below. "Is there a lantern?"

"I never thought to bring one!" Callie peered down. "There's something there, a beam or a support of some sort. Do you see the outline? It's probably holding up this section."

"Well, I can't get this loose. I'll have to cut it." Felix picked up the saw once more and leaned into the opening. "No," he announced the next moment. "It's a beam, all right, but it's just resting on its support. If I shift this—" He gave a mighty shove, and the ancient wood timbers creaked and slid sideways.

The section beneath Tony wavered, then with a splintering crash it gave way, collapsing beneath him, dropping him into the darkness below.

Fourteen

Shocked into immobility, Callie simply stared at the gaping, splintered hole where only a moment before Tony had knelt watching Felix with an expression of mingled consternation and amusement. Lady Agatha, opposite her, sprang to her feet, her face ashen. Marianne let out a soft shriek.

"Tony!" Callie found her voice and lunged forward, still on her hands and knees.

"Don't!" Felix caught her. His horrified gaze met hers. "You might take more of it down on top of him." He looked up at Lady Agatha. "It isn't far," he said with forced certainty. "He'll be all right." Gingerly, he edged closer to the hole.

A groan sounded from below them, followed by Tony's strained voice. "Felix, you are a—"

"There are ladies present," Felix called, cutting him off short. Relief filled his voice. "I presume that beam was not, as I thought, well secured."

"So it would seem," came the dry response. "I—" He broke off on a sharp exclamation of pain.

"Don't move, Tony!" Callie retreated to the other opening where they had pried up the boards. "I'm coming down." When no order issued forth that she was to stay right where she was, she verged on panic. He'd stop her, unless he were so severely injured that he knew he needed her help. He'd— With an effort, she forced down her fear. That wouldn't help him in the least. She had to stay calm and think.

It would be dark down there, she reminded herself. She would have no way of knowing how badly he was hurt. She needed light.

"Marianne, would you fetch a lantern?" Felix voiced the thought uppermost in Callie's mind. His strained gaze remained riveted on the broken hole. "And the footmen, I believe. If you'll have them bring a board, or a gate, we can carry him back to the house."

"A light, certainly," Tony called through gritted teeth. "But I have not yet broken my neck."

"Just the lantern," Callie told Marianne, then lowered her voice. "And warn Mrs. Durstan."

"Meddlesome." Tony tried to make a joke of the word, but it came out on a gasp.

That did it. Callie cast a reassuring smile at Lady Agatha and swung her feet over the lip of their excavation. After rolling to her stomach, she lowered herself with infinite care until the toes of her half boots encountered something jagged but hard. She tested this for stability, then put her weight on it and eased herself down onto what she realized had to be a pile of rocks.

"Tony?" She called his name softly as she peered through the darkness.

"Here. How nice of you to drop in for a visit."

"Idiot." But he sounded reassuringly near. She stooped low so as not to strike her head on the beams, and crawled in the direction of his voice. "Are the rocks piled about everywhere?" she asked, feeling her way with caution.

"They are where I am lying."

The scrapings of his movement reached her, closer now, and the next moment her questing hand closed on buckskin. With a soft cry of relief, she followed this until she found his hand, which reached for her. "Tony," she whispered on a quavering sob. She eased herself nearer until she reached his shoulder, then wrapped her arm about his chest, not daring to hold him as she longed. "How badly are you hurt? And tell me the truth, for once."

His breath caught, and he cursed softly. "I don't know," he managed to get out.

"Well, that's honest, at least." For the briefest moment, her fingers caressed his neck, then moved to feel for damage to his arms and legs.

Footsteps moved above them, carefully avoiding the damaged area, and the silhouette of a head appeared in the space where Callie had entered. "Tony?" called Lady Agatha.

"I haven't killed myself yet," he assured his parent. "But I greatly fear it was I, and not Felix, who destroyed your work of art."

"I don't think he's broken anything," Callie reported, answering his mother's unspoken question. "But I doubt he's done his knee any good. The sooner we get him out of here, the better. Felix? Will you send a groom for the doctor?"

"At once." Shuffling sounds announced his scrambling to his feet.

"Not yet." Tony caught Callie's hand and gave it a reassuring squeeze. "I was more startled than hurt. And since I'm already down here, I'm not leaving until I've had a good look."

"You could come back later," she suggested. "There are other ways of descending, you know."

"Minx. You just want me out of here so you can have the fun of looking without me."

The teasing in his voice sounded forced. Did he refuse to leave out of fear that he might not be able to come back? He didn't say so; possibly, it never occurred to him. But it occurred to Callie. She'd started him on this hunt because she thought it would be good for him, for all the best possible reasons. So how could everything have gone so horribly wrong? That he had injured himself, she couldn't doubt. How badly, though, she had no way of telling. She clung to him, waiting for Marianne to return with the lantern.

"Can you tell if there are many rocks down here?" Tony asked with determined cheerfulness. "Or was I merely lucky in my landing place?"

"I came down onto rock, but I wasn't far from you. Just a moment." With reluctance, she released her hold on him and groped across the rocks, advancing her weight carefully so as not to shift them. For approximately three more feet she encountered the tumbled stones. Then her questing hand encountered cold, damp dirt. "Just lucky," she announced as she returned to him.

They fell silent, waiting, allowing Tony to recover before he would have to move. Then in the distance came the pounding of running feet, and the gasping, guttural voice of Tony's personal groom demanded: "Where's 'is lordship?"

"Grimsby? What the devil are you doing here?" Tony demanded.

"Ah, there you are, m'lord." The breathing remained heavy from the exertion, but the fear faded from his tone. "Might of known as 'ow you'd come a cropper. When 'er ladyship come runnin' to the stable— Well, that's neither 'ere nor there. We'll 'ave you out o' there all right and tight, never you fear."

"What I fear is you talking me to death. Did you bring a lantern?"

"Aye, that I did, m'lord." The clank of metal sounded, followed by some muttered oaths, then boots scraped, and suddenly light filled the darkened cavity as the groom lowered the lantern toward them.

Callie caught it eagerly, thanking the man. She turned at once to Tony, who had managed to prop himself up on one hand. He looked drawn; even by lantern light, his face was unnaturally pale. He bled from several deep scratches, and she had not a doubt he would discover some exceptionally painful bruises before morning. And if that were the extent of the damage, she would consider him incredibly lucky.

He dragged himself into a sitting position, and a spasm of pain crossed his features as he eased his leg straight. "Bring the light here."

Still keeping low, she scrambled back to him. She wanted to look him over more thoroughly, but any attempt, she knew, he would scorn. She settled for surreptitious glances as she held the lantern so he could survey the scene. "Do you see anything? A bag, perhaps?"

"No. Can you shine the light around the foundations?"

She did, but no sign of Henry's hoard did she discover. As she sat back on the rocks at Tony's side, perplexed and disappointed, she caught a glimpse of a very familiar flicker. "Look." She nudged Tony, and pointed. "Anne's here. Which means the treasure must be as well."

"But not out in the open." He frowned. "Why would Henry need to hide it, beyond just setting it down here?" His hand dropped to the stones on which he sat, and a sudden, arrested gleam lit his eyes. He ran his fingers over them, and nodded. "Masonry rubble, wouldn't you say?" It looks rather like the type used in the buttress at the carriage house."

"It does?" She regarded it with skepticism. "It could be, I suppose, though in this light I wouldn't care to wager on it. But what if it is? Henry would hardly haul it over here to dump on his treasure."

"No, but the workmen might well have disposed of it here *after* he hid the treasure."

"And covered it up, without ever realizing

what they did! Felix!" she called, her hopes soaring. "Bring the shovel, will you? I'm going to need help." She turned to regard Tony, who had already slid down to the dirt and was trying to roll one of the heavy stones aside. "I don't suppose—" she began.

"No. Don't even suggest I leave. Would you?"

"I'm not the one who just fell on rocks," she pointed out.

He shook his head, his face spasmed once again, but defiantly he grasped broken stone and muscled it aside. "I'll rest a great deal better if we find our families' fortunes," he said through gritted teeth.

She opened her mouth to tell him he'd only be able to rest at all by the grace of a hefty drought of laudanum, but bit back the words. There were some times, she realized, when it would do more harm than good to argue with him, as much as they both enjoyed the occupation. Instead, she said merely: "At least let us get some help."

He made no protest, so she called down not only Felix but also the stern-looking Grimsby. With a bullying fondness that Tony would never accept from her, the groom maneuvered his master into a position where Tony could do very little. That accomplished, the groom set to work ripping down a portion of flooring. Felix lent a hand, and in a surprisingly short time the late afternoon sun spilled across them and it became possible to stand erect.

Lady Agatha and Marianne crept near the edge, peering inside. "Shall we send for the footmen?" Marianne called.

Tony shook his head. "There isn't enough room for any more workers."

"They can have my place." Felix wiped the begrimed back of his shirt sleeve across his dampened forehead, leaving a muddied streak, then resumed his labors.

In all, it took the better part of half an hour for the four of them to clear the mound of rubble from where it lay. The smaller pieces they lifted, the heavier had to be rolled. Felix took charge of disposing of the stones on the far side of the folly, clearing the way for the others to shift more. Finally, Callie and Tony dragged the last stones aside.

For one hundred years, beneath that seemingly random pile of stone, had lain nothing but smooth earth.

Callie sank to the ground, exhausted, not able to believe the utter failure of their efforts. "I felt so certain . . ." Her words trailed off and she sank her head into her hands.

Tony leaned heavily against the opening in the floor, his countenance pale and strained. "I thought Anne was here."

"Well, no more reason for you to remain, m'lord. Best get you out o' 'ere." Grimsby positioned himself at Tony's side and eyed the flooring above them. "It's about time for them footmen, I think."

Callie closed her eyes. All for naught. That was what Cedric had said, too. All for naught. At least she hadn't murdered Tony in her greed. She'd only caused him incredible pain, and who knew what further damage to his knee. She had raised all their hopes, and they

had nothing to show for their efforts but a ruined floor.

A chill seeped through her, and she shivered.
An otherworldly chill. She raised her head,
wincing at the soreness in her neck and shoulders, and looked about. The frantic flame that
was the ghostly presence of Anne flickered and
danced before her, above the ground they had
cleared.

"Tony?" Callie came to her feet. "Tony!
Anne is still here!"

Tony followed the direction of her pointing
finger, then met her gaze. All traces of weari-
ness fell away from him. "The shovel—"

Callie reached for it, but he grabbed it first.
This time, even the groom made no argument.
They simply stood back to give him room. He
thrust the blade deep into the soft, damp earth,
and an exclamation of satisfaction escaped him.
"There's something here."

"You can't put pressure on that knee." Felix
took the shovel from him and set to work.

Tony took an uneven, hobbling step backwards, and Callie moved to his side, ready to
support him if needed. Once more he leaned
on the flooring, but now his expression of pain
mingled with tension and excitement. It
wrapped about Callie, heightening her own
soaring hopes. As the ghostly flame's dance increased to a frenetic level, Callie held her
breath.

Felix heaved another spadeful of earth from
the growing hole, then abruptly stopped. With
a puzzled frown, he sank to one knee and

reached into the hole to probe. The others started forward.

"Don't!" he exclaimed. "Stay—stay where you are." He swallowed and rubbed his chin with his muddied hand. "Cousin Agatha? I think you should take the ladies back to the house."

"I shall do no such thing!" Tony's mama declared. "What have you found?"

"What is it?" Callie asked at the same time. Ignoring his orders, she peered over his shoulder.

Rotted cloth. His digging had uncovered Henry's treasure bag! Several inches of the brocade material lay exposed, its metal buttons tarnished from damp and age, its sheen mellowed by fraying and—

Buttons?

Callie reeled and fell back a pace, to be caught by Tony's encircling arm.

"What—?" he began.

She shook her head and turned against his shoulder, burying her face against the soft linen of his shirt. His cheek pressed against the side of her forehead, and his hand stroked her hair, soothing. He had comforted her in just this same way when she was a child. She clung to him, fighting back tears, yet could not prevent her gaze from returning to Felix and the horror he had uncovered.

"Cousin Agatha?" Felix repeated, his voice strained. He never took his gaze from his discovery. "Take Marianne to the house. Callie? You should go with them." He turned, his face haggard. "You know what we've found, don't you?"

Callie nodded. "Henry," she whispered.

Marianne shrieked and clung to Lady Agatha. Agatha put an arm about the girl and turned her away. "Tony?" she asked, shaken, looking to her son for direction. "What should we do?"

"Send for the vicar," Tony said. "He seems the most likely to know what's best." His hold tightened on Callie.

"And send out a bottle or two of brandy," Felix suggested. He set the shovel aside. "I'm going to need them."

"That's what Anne wanted." Callie shook her head. "The treasure never concerned her. She only cared about Henry, about our finding his body once we knew the true story."

"We must see to it that he is properly interred in consecrated soil. This is one wrong, at least, we can set partly to rights." Tony eased away from her, and a sharp cry broke from him.

His groom dove to his side, catching Tony's weight as the bad knee buckled on him. "Time to get 'is lordship out o' 'ere. Where'r them footmen?" the wiry little man demanded.

Between them, Grimsby and Felix, with Callie's determined help, eased Tony from beneath the floor. Once laid on the remaining boards, he attempted to rise. Pain shot across his face and he dropped back, breathing hard, perspiration standing out on his dirtied, bloodied face. He made no further attempt to move.

Callie sat at his side, fighting to keep back the tears of misery. It was her fault, this whole, horrid mess. Tony must blame her, too. Everything she had done, everything that had seemed such fun, such a perfect way to roust him from his fit of the blue devils, had turned into an unmitigated disaster.

He would never forgive her for all the trouble she had caused. How could he? If she had two shillings to rub together, she would run away. And she had a strong suspicion Tony would greet the news with heartfelt relief.

Fifteen

Tony stirred from unconsciousness to an impression of complete blackness. He ached all over, and for some reason he couldn't move his left leg. Memory remained hazy, but he had a vivid impression of rifles, of dust swirling in the heat, of the shouting of men and the raw terror of his mount. The effort to move, even to open his eyes, proved too much. Vaguely it registered with him that someone was there, touching his brow, speaking in a soft voice, pressing something damp to his lips. He needed to know if they'd carried the day, what had become of his troops. Uttley had taken a ball; he'd seen him fall. In another moment, he would try again, and demand answers . . .

The next time he roused, the darkness beyond his lids had faded. The sun shone, but on the same day, or another? He lay still, martialing his mental resources before they faded again. The battle—

No, that wasn't right. That had been months ago. His mind refused to cooperate, but this time he recognized the cause, the familiar unpleasant taste in his mouth of laudanum. He'd been drugged. But why?

He'd fallen. From his horse? But he couldn't ride. A carriage accident, then? He'd driven out to check the harvest, and then Callie—

Callie. Thought of her brought memory flooding back. He'd fallen, all right, straight through the floor of the folly, on top of Henry Rycroft's improvised grave. A low groan escaped him, less of pain than of frustration.

"Easy," said the soft voice at his side. A feathery touch smoothed back the hair from his forehead.

He reached up, caught the wrist, then pried open his eyes. "Callie."

She smiled at him, but the effect was unusually somber. "Here, if you'll let me help you, I have water for you."

"I can sit up on my own." Before he could make the attempt, his valet bustled forward from wherever he had been waiting in the room and slipped a sturdy arm about his master to help him into a more upright position. As his weight shifted, Tony felt the unnatural stiffness of his left leg; bandages swathed it from hip to ankle. Sudden pain lanced through it, further exacerbating his temper. "Why the devil did you let that damned sawbones drug me?"

"My lord! In front of Miss?" the elderly valet demanded, outraged. "What your mother would say!" He shook his head.

"Doing it too brown, Fimber." Tony shook his head with care. "You've heard *her* say a great deal worse."

A reminiscent light lit Fimber's eye. "That I have, my lord. Though never in front of Miss."

"The laudanum was the only way we could think of to keep you still for a couple of hours." Callie thrust pillows behind him for support, and some of the strain eased from her expression. "Honestly, Tony, if you don't allow that leg to rest, it will never heal."

"So it is all my own fault, I suppose?" He regarded her with a kindling eye as she stuffed in the last cushion.

Her face clouded again. "No. It is mine, and I am so terribly sorry."

That took him aback. Normally she defended even the most outrageous of her exploits. He'd never before known her to accept blame so docilely. "Are you feeling well?" he demanded with exaggerated concern.

"I am feeling quite wretched. And now," she added as she handed him the water, "I must go and tell your mama you are awake."

He let her go, and nodded to his man that he needed no more assistance. Fimber retreated to the armchair near the hearth, where a discarded blanket indicated he had passed a sleepless night. The elderly Harold sprawled across the carpet, snoring gently. The black and white Archimedes lay curled against the spaniel's stomach. Apparently Tony had had considerable company during the long hours he'd lain oblivious.

Now he wanted time to think, time to assimilate all that had occurred. Callie's attitude troubled him. Had his injuries been no more than merely troublesome, she would have rallied him with a lecture on being more careful, and they would have ended with a rousing argument, and both felt immeasurably better for it. Only she had neither lectured nor argued.

Tentatively, he tried to move his leg, and gasped at the pain that stabbed through him. He collapsed against the pillows, breathing hard, and a fine sheeting of sweat broke out on his brow. Laudanum didn't seem such a bad idea, at the moment.

"Master Tony?" Fimber stood at his side, anxious.

"Just—just being clumsy. What time is it?"

"Gone on ten, now, my lord. The doctor was hoping you'd sleep until noon or later."

"Well, I haven't, and I'm ravenous. Do you think you could find me some breakfast?"

A smile tugged at the elderly valet's mouth. "Shall I ring, or would you rather I went down myself, since that would be faster than ringing? Unless you might need me?"

"At the moment, I need breakfast more."

Fimber hesitated, then seemed to make up his mind. With a last admonition to lie still and not try anything that might aggravate his injury, the valet hurried from the room.

Tony watched the closing of the door, then turned his attention to his leg. How much damage had he done to himself? Sufficient, he feared, to counteract the healing that had taken place since the original injury. He tried to move his toes, and instantly regretted the impulse. Had it, he wondered uneasily, been this bad before?

He stared straight ahead, waiting for the pain

to ease, but it didn't. He drew a deep breath. It *would* pass. It had to. The pain always faded to a dull ache. But not this time.

Not this time. Those words echoed through his mind like a death knell. This time, he might well have to accept the fact that he had done himself an injury too serious to heal. If so, he would be sensible about it. He wouldn't rail against fate and act as if the world had come to an end. He would accept a future of limitations to his activities. He would live, he would go on. He would even, eventually, drag the Grange from its morass of debt. The fact that he had crippled himself would make little difference to anyone but him.

And Callie. It would make a very big difference to her. She knew the extent of his injuries, and she blamed herself. She claimed responsibility.

She would also try to make amends.

Warmth flooded through him, for her loyalty, for her determination. For her damned stubbornness. And he knew what form her remorse would take.

She had never wanted to marry him. She'd agreed to the engagement to satisfy his sense of honor; he'd known that at the time. He'd intended to give her her freedom every bit as much as she'd intended to give him his. But that would change, now.

From guilt, from knowing the reasons he had offered for her in the first place, she would now insist they be wed, and as soon as possible.

He closed his eyes as the vision of this future washed over him. Her self-blame would remain ever-present in her mind, bound there by his presence, a constant reminder of his physical limitations that she believed she caused. She would wilt, her liveliness would be quenched, she would become a drudge from guilt, bound by duty to care for an infirm husband.

And she would never believe that he didn't hold her responsible.

The door opened, and his mother strode in, her face lined with anxiety. He forced a smile and a light greeting, but she made no response. She crossed to the bedside and looked down on him, her worried eyes studying his countenance. Behind her, he glimpsed Callie standing in the doorway.

"You needn't look so solemn." He managed a commendably rallying note. "I've not—er—cocked up my toes, yet."

His mother's nose wrinkled, but she visibly relaxed. "What a very vulgar expression, to be sure. How do you go on?"

"I shall do considerably better once I've had the opportunity to deal with a rare beef steak and a tankard of ale. Fortunately, Fimber is seeing to it."

Marmaduke's orange and white nose appeared from beneath Callie's skirts, followed by the rest of the massive cat as the animal ambled into the room. With a grace belied by its girth, it leapt onto the bed and began kneading the blankets. Tony winced. The other cat stirred against the spaniel, eyes intent on Marmaduke. It rose, stretched, and headed for the bed as well.

"You spoil them," Lady Agatha declared with

more indulgence than disapproval as Archimedes settled on a toppled pillow.

Callie advanced into the room, but only to allow Durstan to enter. The butler looked at once to Tony, his worried gaze taking in the cat-infested bed, and a relieved smile flickered across his otherwise impassive countenance. He turned to Lady Agatha. "Mrs. Leeds is ready to depart, my lady, and has asked that his lordship's carriage be brought around. And the vicar has called. He is waiting in the Gold Salon."

A muttered oath escaped Lady Agatha. "I must go down to them both, I suppose. Calpurnia, do you come?"

"She'll follow in a minute," Tony said before Callie could answer. "If you will stay and talk with me?"

"Of course." Yet it was with noticeable reluctance that Callie resumed the chair she had occupied earlier.

He waited until the others had left, and the door closed firmly behind them, before he turned to her. "I am calling off our engagement," he said without preamble.

Her face paled, but she thrust out her chin. "I thought you might try to do that. I am very sorry to be so disobliging, Tony, but I will not allow you to jilt me."

"I am not jilting you. You know—"

"Jilting me," she repeated, cutting across his words. She held up her hand, displaying the sapphire and gold band. "You definitely gave this to me to mark our betrothal, and betrothed we will remain. I shall not permit you to make a laughingstock of me. Either you marry me," she added in tones that would have done credit to an actress in a Cheltenham tragedy, "or you will find yourself with a breach of promise suit on your hands."

In spite of himself, he felt the old amusement rise, "That might be preferable to living with a termagant like you."

"Oh, no. You shouldn't like the scandal at all," she assured him. "Every gossip-monger in town would have their version to tell of your seducing and betraying a mere child who had fallen into your evil clutches, and—"

"Callie, you wretch—" He couldn't help but grin. "Now, do be sensible for once. You must see I am not the husband for you. And I don't want any argument," he added as she opened her mouth in indignant protest.

She straightened, the image of outrage. "Argue? Me? When have I ever argued with you?"

Wisely, he ignored that. "I'll not have you make a sacrifice of yourself, is that understood? You don't want to marry me, and you know it."

An odd expression flickered across her face, only to vanish the next moment. "I don't?"

"You don't," he repeated firmly. "You will stay here, of course, until I have matters well enough in hand to be able to settle some money on you. You will have a Season, that I promise. And you will find a husband worthy of you."

She stared at him for a long moment. "Worthy of me."

He closed his eyes. "You know what I mean, Callie. A husband who can dance with you and ride with you, who will be able to give you all you deserve. A husband you can love, not just marry out of pity or for convenience."

She regarded him searchingly, opened her mouth, then closed it again. After a long moment, she said slowly, as if testing the waters: "You are quite serious, are you not?"

"I am. I will not let you throw yourself away on me, so let us hear no more nonsense about our being wed. Is that clear?"

"What is clear," she said, reverting to her normal self, "is that you are working yourself into a high fever—"

"I'm not even warm!"

"—and must not be agitated any further. We will continue this discussion after the doctor has been to see you." She rose briskly. "And now I must go down to the vicar. I fear I am poor Henry's only living relative, and must make myself available for consultation." With that, she left the room.

He was still frowning at the door when it opened again, this time to admit Fimber carrying the requested breakfast on a tray.

More than an hour passed before he saw Callie again. By then the doctor had come, inspected his leg, and pronounced himself satisfied. He granted Tony the privilege of removing to a day bed, if one might be set up, and promised to return the following morning. Tony disdained that suggestion and instead, with the hovering aid of Fimber, settled himself in the easy chair before the hearth, his leg supported on a footstool. Feeling less like an invalid, he sent for Bradshaw to hear how the harvest and repairs progressed.

The estate agent had barely arrived when his door burst open once more, and Callie started in, breathing heavily, only to pull up short. Excitement radiated from her. "I beg your pardon, but, Tony, I must speak with you."

Bradshaw rose at once. "If you will excuse me, my lord? There are some matters to which I should attend."

"Of course." Tony studied Callie as she moved away from the door to permit the man to leave.

As soon as he had gone, she hurried forward, hands extended. He grasped them and drew her down to the footstool.

"I saw the ghost again!" She clung to his hands, quivering. "Not Anne, the other one. Tony, it is Henry! Now that I—I have met him in person, so to speak, I am certain of it."

"Henry?" He frowned. "But the last time we saw the other flame, it led us *away* from his body. It was Anne who took us to it."

"It was Henry then, too, radiating a sensation of guilt. I thought it must be Cedric, but now I know it wasn't." Her eyes, wide and bright, watched him. "What could be more important to a ghost than the revealing of his murdered mortal remains?"

"The reason he was murdered," he said slowly. Her enthusiasm wrapped about him, infusing him. "Then perhaps he wasn't leading us away from the folly, but—"

"But *into* the maze, as we thought at the time," Callie finished for him.

"The maze," Tony repeated. "Do you think he could have left it there?" No need to explain what "it" was.

"There is only one way to find out. Will you come with me?"

His enthusiasm evaporated. "I can't."

"Don't be absurd. You are sitting up, are you not? Do you not think you could do so in a Bath chair, if I were to push it with care?"

"A Bath chair!" He spoke the words with loathing, but the idea had possibilities.

"You don't expect me to rely on Felix for help, do you?"

"Good God, no. Would you truly be reduced to that? I suppose I cannot let that happen." He eyed her with sudden suspicion. "I suppose you just happen to know the whereabouts of a Bath chair?"

"Albert found one in the attics last night." Her lips twitched. "Truly, Tony, you mustn't mind. We all knew you would go mad if you were forced to lie abed, and you will only need the chair for a very little while."

A very little while. Was there a chance she might be right? Even if she weren't, even if he were reduced to such means to get about, at least he *would* get about. He would not confine himself to his bed, not when she was here with him, offering him quests and adventures. "Well?" he demanded. "What are you waiting for?"

Getting down the stairs proved the hardest part. Fimber, to his dismay, could not bear Tony's weight, and reluctantly gave way to Albert and James, who made a chair of their arms. With ill grace, Tony submitted to being carried down to the Great Hall. This was accomplished with such solicitude, Tony actually welcomed the wheeled chair and the freedom it provided from his well-wishers.

"Fimber?" Tony signaled to his hovering valet.

The man hurried forward, his countenance every bit as strained as if he had just made the difficult journey himself. "Yes, Master Tony?"

"Have I been reduced to that?" Tony murmured. "Will you have one of the unused rooms made up for me down here? I have no desire to exhaust us all every time I wish for a change of scenery."

The valet looked relieved. "Very good, my lord."

Albert moved forward to push the chair, but Callie waved him back. "I can manage," she assured him. "And I think poor Fimber will be grateful for all the help he can get."

"You do not want anyone else in on this, do you?" Tony murmured as she trundled him toward the library and its easy access to the terrace.

"Not until we know for certain. I fear the staff is beginning to think we are both quite mad."

"We are," came his prompt response. "Where did you see this ghost?"

"By the hedge, where we saw it before."

"Did you follow it?"

"That wouldn't have been fair, not after all the trouble I have caused you. If we might really find Henry's treasure, then you should be there, too."

They emerged onto the terrace to find the grooms busily engaged in laying planks along the steps leading down to the garden. Grimsby sprang forward and eased the Bath chair down the ramp, admonishing Callie all the while to stay to the verge rather than try to push the contraption along the gravel. He would have accompanied them, ignoring Tony's thanks and dismissal, had Callie not begged him to see to the erection of such ramps at other likely sites.

"*More* ramps?" he demanded as the wiry groom set off with a zealous gleam in his eyes. "You don't know what you have unleashed. I can see I am going to have to rid myself of this thing if I am ever to enjoy a moment's peace."

"The doctor implied a week at most, and less if you behave yourself."

"A week?" Hope surged, only to fade. "Don't trifle with me, Callie."

"I would do no such thing." For once, her voice remained serious. "Your knee is bruised and swollen, but that will go away."

"And after that?" At her silence, he added: "He doesn't know, does he? I could be crippled."

"If you want to be. I think it would be far more entertaining to return to your old self, do not you? Oh, I doubt you will want to stand up for more than one dance at a time, but then you never did anyway, that I recall. You always complained about balls."

"What I complained about, as I remember,

was the way you trod on my feet when you begged me to help you practice."

"Well, that was better than listening to you torturing the poor pianoforte while Oliver danced with me." They reached the end of the hedge and she guided the chair onto the moss and stone pathway between the maze's walls.

Almost at once, a chill settled over him. Callie slowed, her tension palpable. "You feel it?" he asked. He strained to see ahead into the shadowed turns, searching for a glimpse of the ghostly flame.

It eluded them. Callie strained forward with the chair over the soft moss, navigating the passages as quickly as she could. Tony clung to the arms, much preferring to move under his own power. But now, the only thing that mattered was to find the specter and discover where—if anywhere—it led them.

They negotiated the final turn, advanced along the leafy corridor, and emerged into the central clearing. Everything remained the same, no flickering flames danced above the fountain or darted in and out of the tiny gazebo against the shrubs beyond it. The benches lining the area— Satisfaction rushed through him. One of them glowed with a shimmering, unearthly light.

"There," he breathed. He dragged himself up.

Callie shoved him back, gently but firmly. "You cannot. Not yet, at least. Stay where you are, for heaven's sake, or you'll never be rid of this thing." She started forward, leaving him there, and dropped to her knees beside the bench.

The flame flickered above it, hovering near, as if it waited, as it must have waited for a hundred years.

Callie pushed. Tony, gritting his teeth at his impotence, watched her strain against the stone slab that rested on massive supports. With a grating screech, the top inched aside at an angle.

She peered in, then sank back on her heels. "It's empty," she called, and repositioned herself at the other side and pushed again. At first nothing happened, then the grating resumed and the slab moved inexorably backward. Breathing heavily from her efforts, she looked inside.

A soft exclamation escaped her. She reached in, then turned back to him, holding aloft with some effort a bulky, mildewed bag of soft leather. She ran to the chair and fell on her knees before Tony, laughing, tears of triumph slipping down her cheeks. "We have it!" she cried.

Tony, in disbelief, held out his hands. She dragged off the cord that held it closed and, grasping the weighty bag with both hands, poured some of the contents across his hands and lap. Glittering gems, dulled coins, golden chains fell across his palms. She dropped the sack, staring at their discovery, and reached out with a tentative finger to touch a large ruby brooch.

"The Rycroft fortune," Tony breathed.

"And the Lambeth," Callie pointed out. Her

gaze remained riveted in awe. "They seem to be intermingled."

He shook his head. "I'll grant you the lot. For what my ancestors did to yours, we owe you that."

"It belongs to us both," she announced with decision. She opened the neck of the bag that lay at her side and drew out a necklace of emeralds set with gold and pearls. "There's so much here! Tony, there's enough for you to repair the farms and pay off Reginald's debts. And enough to give Felix and Marianne a stake so they may start their gaming house in Munich or Paris or wherever they want."

"And enough," Tony added, "so you will have no need for a marriage of convenience." In spite of his efforts, he couldn't keep the hollow note from his voice.

She sat back on her heels, unblinking, staring at him. "I never had any such intention. I marry for love, or not at all."

"Then that's settled, then." He fought against the bleakness that threatened to overwhelm him

"Of course it is settled. We settled it days ago, when you gave me this." She held up the hand and displayed the sapphire ring once more.

He fought the ragings of longing and shook his head. "You cannot love the wreck of a man. You deserve so much more."

"There, we are in complete agreement. I do deserve more. I deserve you."

"Callie—"

She held her finger to his lips, silencing him.

"Are you going to sit there and tell me you don't love me?"

"Are you going to let me speak?"

"If you try, I shan't believe you. I thought you didn't, of course, but everything you have said today proves that you do, even if you are not aware of it."

"Callie—" He broke off and drew a steadying breathe. Of course he loved her, damn it! He had always loved her, always would love her. "We are friends," he pronounced with a firmness he hoped she would accept as final.

"You absolute idiot." She shook her head. "You love me, and you intend to be noble and refuse to marry me."

"I don't love you," he lied.

"You are just trying to think of what's best for me, aren't you? Don't you realize, my beloved idiot, that *you* are what's best for me?"

He started to protest, but she half rose and caught the back of his neck with one hand and drew his head to hers. Her soft mouth found his, clinging, and suddenly nothing mattered but the warmth and love that enveloped him. He grasped her, and the jewels and coins fell unheeded to the ground as he half lifted her, even as she came willingly to him. Her slight weight settling in his lap drove rational thought from his mind. For a very long while he clasped her close, his mouth exploring hers, then moving to brush desire-filled kisses across her eyes and down her slender throat.

She pulled back at last, one hand on his chest, the other still wrapped about his shoulders. She regarded him with eyes tender, her expression filled with wonder—and concern. "Am I hurting you?"

"Only when you stop." Not one to let an opportunity slip, he kissed her again.

"Idiot." The word came out on a shaky laugh. "I shouldn't be sitting on you."

"I don't know about that." He repositioned her slightly, finding her weight both light and delightful. "Actually, it is a pity the chair is only temporary. I am finding it has definite possibilities. And now, my adored little love, you are quite certain about this?"

She answered in the most direct manner possible, and he found her argument utterly convincing. When he could speak again, he said: "I have no desire to postpone our wedding until I have healed enough to dance."

"As I remember your rendition of a reel, that is probably for the best," she murmured.

"We will dance later," he continued with ruthless determination. "I only intend to allow the banns to be read instead of obtaining a special license in order to give you time to shop. You will undoubtedly wish to purchase a trousseau suitable to your new status as heiress."

"You are being absurd, as always." She kissed him. "The only status I am interested in is that of your wife. And if it is the cost of a special license that worries you, I believe we can afford it now. In fact—" She broke off. "Tony," she breathed, and pointed toward the center of the maze.

The ghostly light flickered over the stone bench. No, not one, but two of them, he realized. Anne and Henry, reunited once more now that they had completed their earthly tasks. Tony held Callie close as the spectral flames swirled and intermingled, broke apart only to join again in a dance of love so intense the heat of it washed over them. As the specters combined a final time, their glow burned with sudden fury. The sparks flared and shot skyward, united, the spirits freed at last from their ghostly bondage.

"They're gone," Callie said softly.

"Not completely." Tony rested his chin against her forehead. "Can't you feel it? That lingering sensation of love?"

"And what," she demanded, eyes kindling, "makes you think that comes from them and not from us?"

"Minx." He grinned, his arms tightening about her. "I should have known you'd argue with me at the first opportunity."

Her ready smile flashed. "Would you have it any other way?"

"I would not." He kissed her, lingeringly, savoring the rush of sensations as she pressed closer against him. "I'm beginning," he murmured, "to regret the time it will take to procure that special license."

Her love-filled gaze rested on him. "Idiot," she whispered in pure contentment.

Epilogue

The late April sunlight slanted through the bedroom window of Lambeth House, Cavendish Square. Callie, curled up in an overstuffed chair, set precise stitches in the soft muslin of a christening robe, stopping frequently to admire her handiwork. More than four months remained until the birth of Marianne and Felix's first child; she had all the time she needed.

The door opened, and Tony looked in, his smile warming as he caught sight of her. "Well, my minx?"

"You're back!" She sprang to her feet, casting the embroidery aside.

Tony crossed the room in five steps, only the slightest trace of a limp slowing him. Gathering her into a crushing embrace, he kissed her thoroughly, then held her close. "Have you missed me, love?"

"Mmmm. You've been away for ages! How is everything at the Grange?"

"Even better than expected. The last of the repairs are completed, and Bradshaw is in alt over the changes in the crop plans. Only I confess to missing Anne's ghostly presence. How have you fared here?"

"Oh, thanks to your mama, we have been gay to dissipation. If we are not at some Italian breakfast, then it's an *al fresco* picnic or a ball, or the opera." She fought back a yawn, then laughed. "I never thought enjoying oneself could be so exhausting."

His lips brushed her forehead. "Let us dine at home. Here, in your room, if you should like. I rather fancy the thought of retiring early tonight."

She warmed at the promise of his words, but shook her head. "We are pledged to Marianne and Felix. They hoped you might return on time. Did you forget? Tonight is the night they are opening the *rouge et noire*. All the world will flock to St. James's Street."

"All except me," he declared with a firmness that denied argument. "Not even for such an event will I endure the company of Marianne's mama. How they can bear having her live with them—"

"Theirs is a very elegant—and spacious—establishment. Besides, she won't be gracing the gaming rooms tonight. I have it on good authority she will be at the opera. In the box of the earl of Schofield, no less." She fought back another yawn.

Tony's eyebrows rose. "Schofield? Good God. I thought he'd become a complete recluse. What brings him to London?"

"Marianne's mama. It seems she wrote him such a sympathetic and apologetic letter when Marianne refused to marry him, that he decided he'd rather wed the mother than the daughter. Being in London has quite restored him, though he lays that entirely to Mrs. Leeds's tender ministrations. They are to be wed in the middle of next month."

"It seems I must go, then, if only to hear the full tale from Marianne." He frowned as Callie yawned again. "Are you feeling quite the thing? I've never known you to be so tired."

"That's only because I've never been in the family way, before. It's quite natural to be sleepy, I am told. Really, Tony, there's not the least need to stare at me with that perfectly idiotish expression. It's— Tony!" she exclaimed as he swept her off her feet.

"Minx!" he breathed against her hair. "You might have told me at once! Are you well?"

"Except for being in imminent danger of being crushed!" she protested. "Be careful of him."

He swung her into his arms, then sank onto the edge of the bed, settling her on his lap. A stunned look lingered in his eyes. "Him? Are you so certain you're carrying my heir?"

She nodded in mock solemnity. "Your mama has ordered it so. She insists I produce a little boy, exactly like you."

"I would be satisfied with a little girl," he vowed, "just like you. Complete," he added, recovering a trifle, "with your temper."

A choke of laughter escaped her as he lowered her to the bed, his mouth seeking hers. "I'll remind you of that," she murmured when she could speak again, "next time we argue."

"Us? Argue?" His lips brushed with a feathery touch along her throat. "You shock me."

Her arms crept around his neck as she pulled him down to her. "Beloved idiot," she whispered, and kissed him.

BOOK YOUR PLACE ON OUR WEBSITE AND MAKE THE READING CONNECTION!

We've created a customized website just for our very special readers, where you can get the inside scoop on everything that's going on with Zebra, Pinnacle and Kensington books.

When you come online, you'll have the exciting opportunity to:

- View covers of upcoming books

- Read sample chapters

- Learn about our future publishing schedule (listed by publication month *and author*)

- Find out when your favorite authors will be visiting a city near you

- Search for and order backlist books from our online catalog

- Check out author bios and background information

- Send e-mail to your favorite authors

- Meet the Kensington staff online

- Join us in weekly chats with authors, readers and other guests

- Get writing guidelines

- AND MUCH MORE!

Visit our website at
http://www.zebrabooks.com

WATCH FOR THESE REGENCY ROMANCES

LOOK FOR THESE REGENCY ROMANCES

SCANDAL'S DAUGHTER   (0-8217-5273-1, $4.50)
by Carola Dunn

A DANGEROUS AFFAIR   (0-8217-5294-4, $4.50)
by Mona Gedney

A SUMMER COURTSHIP   (0-8217-5358-4, $4.50)
by Valerie King

TIME'S TAPESTRY   (0-8217-5381-9, $4.99)
by Joan Overfield

LADY STEPHANIE   (0-8217-5341-X, $4.50)
by Jeanne Savery